the
heart-
keeper

FRANÇOISE SAGAN

the heart-keeper

FRANÇOISE SAGAN

Translated from the French by
Robert Westhoff

E. P. DUTTON & CO., INC.
NEW YORK   1968

To Jacques

the
heart-
keeper

The earth hath bubbles, as
the water has.

SHAKESPEARE

1

The road bordering the ocean at Santa Monica stretched out straight, relentless, under Paul's purring Jaguar. It was warm, and the humid air smelled of gasoline and the night. Paul was driving ninety miles an hour. He had taken on the casual look of those who drive too fast; on his hands he wore gloves neatly opened at the knuckles, like those of racing drivers, which made his hands seem to me slightly repugnant.

My name is Dorothy Seymour—forty-five years old, features a bit worn, because nothing in my life has seriously prevented it. I am a screen writer—a rather successful one—and still very attractive to men, probably because they attract me, too. I am one of those dreadful exceptions that shame Hollywood: at twenty-five I was, as an actress, a smash hit in an art film; at twenty-six I left Hollywood to squander my earnings with a leftist painter in Europe. At twenty-seven I returned to Hollywood—an unknown, without a dollar, and with several lawsuits on my hands. Since I was no longer solvent, the studio stopped the proceedings and decided to employ me as a screen writer, the sound of my glorious name no longer making an impression on the ungrateful public. I was rather pleased; the autographs, photographers, and awards had always bored me. I became "The One Who Could Have" (like some Indian chief). . . . Furthermore, my good health and fertile imagination, both due to an Irish grandfather, finally earned me a certain reputation for the output of stupidities in color —highly remunerative, it seems, to my astonishment. The historical epics of RKB, for example, often carry my credit line, and in my nightmares I sometimes see Cleopatra approaching, declaring bitterly, "No, Madam, I did not say, 'Pass, O sovereign of my heart,' to Caesar."

Meanwhile, the sovereign of my heart, of my body at least, was to be Paul Brett that evening, and I yawned in advance.

Paul Brett is nevertheless a very handsome man. He represents the interests of RKB and various other film companies. He is elegant, pleasant, and has the face of a choirboy. So much so that Pamela Chris and Lola Crevette, the two biggest sex symbols of our generation, they who for ten years on the screen have devoured men's fortunes and their hearts, and even their own cigarette holders, became successively infatuated with him and collapsed in tears after the breakups. So Paul had a glorious past. But looking at him that evening, despite the circumstances, I saw only a little blond boy—a little blond boy in his forties. Which is depressing. But it had to be done: after eight days of flowers, telephone calls, innuendoes, and going out together, a woman of my age owes it to herself to give in, at least in this country. D-Day had arrived; we sped along at ninety miles an hour toward my modest abode, at two in the morning, and for once I bitterly deplored the importance of sexual relations in a person's behavior. I was sleepy. But I had already been sleepy the night before and three nights before that, so I no longer had the right to be. Paul's understanding, "Of course, darling," would be replaced by the inevitable, "Dorothy, what's happening? You can tell me. . . ." So I would have the happy task of taking the ice cubes from the refrigerator, looking for a bottle of scotch, handing Paul a glass while making the ice cubes tinkle gaily, and at last, reclining in a seductive Paulette Goddard pose on the large sofa in the living room. With that, Paul would come toward me, kiss me, and say afterward, his manner intense: "That was bound to happen, wasn't it, darling?" Yes, it was bound to happen.

I gave a horrible gasp. And Paul, a stifled cry. In the headlights, looming up like a lunatic, or rather like one of those disjointed straw scarecrows I had seen in France, a man plunged toward me. I must say that my little blond boy had remarkable reflexes. He slammed on the brakes and the car swerved into the ditch on the right at the same time as his lovely companion—I am speaking of myself. I found myself, after a series of strange visions, with my nose in the grass, and holding onto my handbag: a curious thing, because I generally forget it everywhere. (What reflex made me grasp that little pouch when faced with what should have been a fatal accident, I'll never know.) Still I heard Paul's voice pronounce my name with an anguish that was flattering, and reassured about him, I shut my eyes again, more than relieved. The lunatic had not been touched. I was intact, so was Paul, and with the formalities to be carried out, the nervous shock, etc., there was a good chance of my sleeping alone that night. "Everything is all right, Paul," I murmured in a dying voice and sat down comfortably in the grass.

"Praise be to God!" cried Paul, who liked to use old, romantic expressions. "Praise be to God, you're not hurt, darling! I thought for a moment . . ."

I don't know what he had thought for a moment, since the next moment, in a hellish racket, we were rolling tangled in a wild embrace ten yards from our ditch. Half deaf, blind, and slightly irritated, I disengaged myself from his arms to see the Jaguar burning like a torch—a well-insured torch, I hoped for his sake. Paul in turn sat up.

"My God," he said, "the gasoline!"

"Is there anything left that could explode?" I asked with a touch of ill humor.

And suddenly I remembered the existence of the lunatic. Maybe he was burning at that very moment. I sprang up, noticing as I got to my feet that I had runs in both of my stockings, and ran toward the road. Paul followed me. A shadowy figure was sprawled on the macadam, sheltered from the fire, but motionless. At first I saw only brown hair that the fire tinged red, then I turned him over without effort and saw a man's face that resembled that of a child.

Don't misunderstand me. I have never loved, do not love, will never love very young men, those they call *minets* in Europe. Their growing popularity—with many of my friends, among others—seemed amazing to me. Almost Freudian. Brats who still smell of milk have no business nestling in the arms of women who smell of scotch. And yet, this face turned toward me on the road, in the light of the flames, this face, young but already so hard, in its perfection filled me with a curious sentiment. I wanted to run away from him, yet at the same time to cradle him in my arms. And I have no maternal complex. My daughter, whom I adore, lives in Paris, happily married, with a flock of little imps that she can only think of passing off on me in the summer, when I take a notion to spend a month on the Riviera. Thank God, I rarely travel alone and so I can blame my maternal short-comings on a sense of decency. To return to that night, and to Lewis—for the lunatic, the scarecrow, the unconscious man, the handsome face, was called Lewis—I stood there an instant before him, motion-less, without even placing my hand on his heart to verify whether he was alive. It seemed unimportant to me, looking at him, whether he was alive or dead. Doubtless an inconceivable sentiment and one that I would bitterly regret later, but not in the sense that one might think.

"Who is it?" Paul said severely.

If there is something admirable about Hollywood people, it is their mania for knowing or recognizing everyone. Paul thought it disagreeable not to be able to call by his name the man he had almost run over in the middle of the night. I became exasperated.

"We're not at a cocktail party, Paul. Do you think he's injured? . . . Oh! . . ."

The brown that was running under the stranger's head, and onto my hands, was blood. I recognized its heat, its sticky contact, its terrifying smoothness. Paul saw it at the same time as I.

"I didn't touch him," he said. "I'm sure of that. He must have been hit by a piece of the car when it exploded."

He stood up; he had a calm, firm voice. I began to understand Lola Crevette's tears.

"Don't move, Dorothy, I'm going to telephone."

He strode off toward the black shadows of the houses farther on. I stayed alone on the road, kneeling beside this man who could be dying. Suddenly he opened his eyes, looked at me, and smiled.

2

"Dorothy, are you completely crazy?"

That is the kind of question I have the hardest time answering. Besides, it was asked by Paul who, wearing an elegant dark blue blazer, looked at me sternly. We were on the terrace of my house and I was dressed for gardening: old canvas slacks, flowered blouse, and a kerchief around my hair. Not that I have ever done any gardening; the mere sight of a pair of pruning shears frightens me, but I like to disguise myself. So every Saturday evening I dress up for gardening, like my neighbors, but instead of following a mad lawnmower over the grass or weeding a rebellious flower bed, I settle down on the terrace with a double whiskey, a book in my hand. It was in this occupation that Paul surprised me. I felt guilty and untidy, two almost equally violent sensations.

"Do you know everyone in town is talking about your latest extravagance?"

"Everyone, everyone," I repeated with a manner as incredulous as modest.

"What in God's name is that boy doing here?"

"But he's recovering, Paul, he's recovering. After all, his leg was badly torn up. And you know he hasn't a dollar, or a family, or anything."

Paul took a deep breath.

"That's exactly what worries me, my dear. Including the fact that your young hippie was full of LSD when he threw himself under my car."

"Look, Paul, he explained that to you himself. Under the influence of his little drugs, he neither recognized nor saw you as an automobile. He thought the headlights were . . ."

Suddenly Paul turned red.

"I don't care what he thought! That imbecile, that little hoodlum almost killed us, and two days after that you bring him to your house, you settle him in your guest room, and you carry him his meals. What if he kills you some day, taking you for a chicken or God knows what? What if he runs off with your jewels?"

(17

I struck back.

"Look, Paul, nobody has ever taken me for a chicken. As for my jewels, they're not much, they're not worth a fortune. After all, we can't leave him on the street, practically an invalid, too."

"You could have left him in the hospital."

"He thought the hospital was dismal and I must say it was."

Paul looked discouraged and sat down in the rattan chair facing me. He mechanically took my glass and drank half its contents. Even though irritated, I didn't stop him. He was obviously at his wits' end. He looked at me strangely.

"Have you been gardening?"

I nodded affirmatively, several times. It is curious to note that certain men continually force you to lie to them. I simply could not explain my innocent Saturday occupations to Paul. He would have called me crazy all over again, and I was beginning to wonder if he was not right.

"You wouldn't notice it," he continued, glancing all around.

My miserable bit of garden was, in fact, a jungle. But I assumed an air of annoyance.

"I do what I can," I said.

"What have you got in your hair?"

I ran my hand through my hair and found two or three wood shavings, white and thin as leaves. I was surprised.

"They're shavings," I said.

"So I see very well," said Paul dryly. "What's more, there are quite a few on the ground, too. Besides gardening, have you taken up carpentry?"

At that moment, a shaving floated down from above and landed on his head. I raised my eyes abruptly.

"Oh! yes," I said, "I know. It's Lewis carving a head in wood, on his bed, to pass the time."

"And he graciously sends his parings down by the window? It's charming."

I started to feel a little nervous, too. Perhaps I was wrong to bring Lewis here, but after all, it was a charitable temporary arrangement with no ulterior motive. And Paul had no rights over me. I decided to point that out to him. He replied that he had the rights over me that every man has over an unthinking woman; that is, the duty to protect her, and more such nonsense. . . . We argued, he left furious, and I remained in my rattan chair, overcome with fatigue, and with a warm whiskey. It was six o'clock in the evening. The shadows lengthened on the lawn littered with leaves, and my evening looked flat, my battle with Paul depriving me of the party we were to have gone to together. There was still the television, which usually bores me, and the few grunts Lewis uttered when I brought him his dinner. I had never seen anyone so quiet. The only time he had spoken distinctly was when he announced his decision to leave the hospital two days after the accident, and he had accepted my hospitality as something to be expected. I was in very good spirits that day, too good, perhaps; it was one of those moments—rare, thank heaven—when you feel every man is at the same time your brother and your child, and you have to take care of him. Since then, I had cared for Lewis, sprawled on a bed at my house, his leg wrapped in bandages that he changed himself. He never read, listened to the radio, or talked. From time to time he would fashion some strange object out of the dry branches that I brought up from the garden. Or he stared out of the window, his face expressionless. Indeed, I asked myself if he were not really an idiot, and this idea, combined with his good looks, seemed most romantic to me. As for my few timid questions about his past, his future, his life, they always brought the same reply: "It isn't interesting." He had found himself on the road one night, in front of our car, his name was Lewis, and that was all. In the meantime, I thought it very restful: long stories tire me and God knows most people don't spare me.

I went into my kitchen, whipped up a delicious dinner out of cans, and climbed the stairs. I knocked on Lewis's door, entered, and put the tray on his bed, which was strewn with shavings. Thinking of the one that had landed on Paul's head, I began to laugh. Lewis raised his eyes, looking intrigued. He had eyes like a cat, very pale blue-green under the black eyelashes, and I thought mechanically that with that look Columbia would sign him up without a second thought.

"You're laughing?"

He had a low voice, a little hoarse, hesitating.

"I'm laughing because Paul got one of your wood shavings on the head, by the window, and he was indignant!"

"Was he badly hurt?"

I looked at him, amazed. It was the first time he had joked, or at least I hoped he was joking. I gave a silly laugh and suddenly felt terribly uncomfortable. After all, Paul was right. What was I doing with this young nut, alone in an isolated house, on a Saturday night? I might have been dancing or laughing with friends, or even making love with my dear Paul or someone. . . .

"You're not going out?"

"No," I replied bitterly. "Am I bothering you?"

The moment that I said it I was sorry. It was contrary to all the laws of hospitality. But Lewis, lying there, began to laugh, a childish laugh, cordial, happy. Suddenly he was his age, suddenly he had a soul, just by virtue of that laugh.

"Are you terribly bored?"

The question caught me off guard. Does one know whether one is terribly bored, a bit bored, or merely bored without fully realizing it, in this strange mess that is life?

"I don't have time to be," I replied stiffly. "I'm a screen writer at RKB, and I . . ."

"Over there?"

A movement of his chin toward the left vaguely indicated the sparkling bay of Santa Monica, Beverly Hills, that vast suburb of Los Angeles, the studios and production offices, and included them all in the same contempt. Perhaps the word contempt is a bit strong, but it was worse than indifference.

"Yes, over there. That's how I make my living."

I was annoyed. In three minutes' time, because of this stranger, I had been made to feel first cheap, then useless. For, as a matter of fact, where was this stupid job leading me except to a little wad of dollars raked together every month and, for that matter, spent every month? Nevertheless, it was indecent to harbor that guilty feeling because of a youngster who was certainly incompetent, and subscribed to LSD. I have nothing against such drugs, but I do not like that they transform one's taste into a philosophy, almost always contemptible, against those who do not participate.

"Make a living," he repeated dreamily. "Make a living."

"It's in style," I said.

"What a shame! I'd like to have lived in Florence in the days when there were plenty of people who took care of the others, like that, for nothing."

"They took care of sculptors or painters or writers. Are you one of those?"

He shook his head.

"Perhaps they took care of people who pleased them, too, for nothing," he said.

I laughed cynically, very Bette Davis.

"You could easily find that here, right now."

I made the same motion with my chin, toward the left, as he had a moment before. He closed his eyes.

"I said 'for nothing.' And that's not 'nothing.' "

There was such feeling in his voice as he said "that" that suddenly I was asking myself all sorts of questions about him, each question more romantic than the last. What did I know about him? Had he loved anyone to the point of madness—at least what they call madness—which has always seemed to me the only sensible way to be in love? Was it really chance, the drug, or despair that had thrown him under the wheels of the Jaguar? Was he healing—resting—his heart at the same time as his leg? And when he looked stubbornly up at the sky, did he see someone's face there? An appalling reflex reminded me that I had used that last formula when I wrote *The Life of Dante*, a production in color, when I was having great trouble in working in a touch of the erotic. The sound of an off-stage voice. Dante, sitting at a rustic, medieval desk, raised his eyes from a tattered manuscript, and the voice murmured:

"When he looked stubbornly up at the sky, did he see someone's face?" A question that the spectators had to resolve themselves, anyway, and I hope in the affirmative.

So it had got to the point where I thought the way I wrote. That would have delighted me if I had had the least literary pretensions or the slightest talent. Too bad . . . I glanced at Lewis. He had opened his eyes and was staring at me.

"What's your name?"

"Dorothy, Dorothy Seymour. Didn't I tell you?"

"No."

I was sitting on the end of his bed. The evening air came in at the window, air filled with the smell of the sea, a smell so strong, so immutable now after all the years I had breathed it, that it was almost cruel in its constancy. How much longer would I voluptuously breathe this air? How long before there would be only nostalgia for the years gone by, the kisses, a man's warmth? I should marry Paul. I should abandon this unlimited confidence in my good health, my mental balance. It is easy to feel good about yourself when someone wants you—but afterward? Yes, afterward? Afterward there would doubtless be the psychiatrists, and the very idea nauseated me.

"You look sad," Lewis said, and he took my hand and looked at it. I too looked at it. We both looked at my hand with a common interest that was laughable, unexpected. He looked at it because he did not know it, and I because it took on another aspect in his hand: it seemed to be an object, it no longer belonged to me. No one had ever held my hand in such an unembarrassed way.

"How old are you?" he asked.

To my great surprise, I heard myself answer truthfully.

"Forty-five."

"You're lucky," he said.

I looked at him, astonished. He must be twenty-six, perhaps less.

"To have gotten that far. That's something well done."

He let go my hand, or rather (as it seemed to me) returned it to my wrist. Then he turned his head and closed his eyes.

"Good night, Lewis," I said, getting up.

"Good night," he said softly. "Good night, Dorothy Seymour."

I shut the door quietly and went down to the terrace. I felt strangely well.

3

"You know that I'll never forget you. I'll never be able to forget you."

"One can forget anything."

"No. There has been something merciless between us, you feel it, too. You . . . must understand. It's not possible that you don't understand."

I interrupted this exciting dialogue, my latest masterpiece, and cast a questioning glance at Lewis. He raised his eyebrows, smiled.

"Do you believe in things being merciless?" he asked.

"It isn't about me; it's about Franz Liszt and . . ."

"But you?"

I began to laugh. I knew that life had sometimes seemed merciless to me and some of my love affairs had left me sure that I would never get over them. And here I was, at forty-five, in my garden, in a very good humor, and not in love with anyone.

"I did believe in them," I said. "And you?"

"Not yet."

He shut his eyes. Little by little, we had begun to talk, about him, about me, about our lives. When I got home from the studio in the evening, Lewis would come down from his room, leaning on two canes, stretch out in the rattan chair, and over a few glasses of scotch we would watch the night come on. When I came home I was glad to find him there, calm, strange, gay and taciturn at the same time, like some unknown creature. Glad, nothing more. I was in no sense in love with him, and strangely, his very handsomeness would have frightened and almost repelled me. I don't know why: he was too smooth, too slender, too perfect. Not at all feminine, but he made me think of the chosen race of which Proust speaks: his hair seemed to be of feathers, his skin of silk. In short, he had nothing of the childish crudeness I found attractive in a man. I even wondered if he shaved, if he needed to shave.

According to himself, Lewis came from a puritan family in New England. After some vague studies, he had set off on foot, done the odd jobs a young man on the road does, and finally ended up in San Francisco. A meeting with others of his own kind, too strong a dose of LSD, a spin in a car, and a fight had led him to where he was: here, with me. When he was well, he would leave—for where, he had no idea. Meanwhile, we talked about life, about art—he was cultured, but with enormous gaps—in short, our relations were such that most people would have considered them highly civilized but at the same time the most unusual that two people could possibly have. But if he questioned me incessantly about my past love affairs, Lewis never spoke of his own; and that was the only shadow—at least, the most alarming one in a boy of his age. He spoke of "men" and "women" in the same tone, detached and flat. And I who, at my age, could not say "men" without an inflection of tenderness, without a gentle and confused surge of memory, sometimes felt cold and indecent.

"When did you first have this feeling of 'merciless'?" Lewis asked. "When your first husband left you?"

"My God, no. I was more or less relieved. Imagine, abstract art, all the time, all the time. . . . But when Frank left, then, yes, I was like a sick animal."

"Who is Frank? The second?"

"Yes, the second. He was nothing exceptional, but he was so gay, so gentle, so happy. . . ."

"And he left you?"

"Lola Crevette became infatuated with him."

(28

He raised his eyebrows, intrigued.

"Surely you've heard of the actress called Lola Crevette?"

He made a vague gesture with his hand. It irritated me but I let it pass.

"To make a long story short, Frank was flattered, in the clouds, and he left me to marry her. At the time, like Marie d'Agoult, I thought I would never recover. For more than a year. Does that surprise you?"

"No. What's become of him?"

"Lola became infatuated with someone else two years later and dropped him. He did three turkeys in a row and took to drink. End of story."

There was silence for a moment. Lewis groaned feebly and tried to get up from his rocking chair.

"Anything wrong?" I asked, alarmed.

"It's painful," he said. "I feel as if I'd never walk again."

For a second I saw myself spending the rest of my days with him, an invalid, and, curiously, the idea seemed neither absurd nor disagreeable. Perhaps I had reached the age to take on a burden. After all, I had not done badly; I had resisted well and for a long time.

"Stay here where you are," I said gaily, "and when your teeth drop out I'll cook your porridge."

"And why will my teeth drop out?"

"It seems that's what happens when one stays in a

horizontal position too long. I must admit it's para-doxical. They really should fall out when one is verti-cal, the law of gravity and all. But no."

He looked at me sideways, a little like Paul, but friendlier.

"You're something," he said. "You know that I could never have left you."

With that, he shut his eyes, asked softly for some poetry, and I went to the library to find something that would please him. It was another of our rituals. I recited in a calm, low voice, in order not to awaken or shock him, Garcia Lorca's "Ode to Walt Whitman":

Heaven has shores for our flights out of life,
*and the corpse need not make itself over at dawn.**

* From *The Poet in New York*, translated by Ben Belitt (New York: Grove Press, 1955).

4

I was in the midst of my work when I got the news. To be exact, I was dictating to my secretary the breathtaking dialogue between Marie d'Agoult and Franz Liszt, as I imagined it, though with no enthusiasm, because I had found out the day before that it was Nodin Duke who would play the part of Liszt, and it was difficult to picture that swarthy bruiser in the role. But in the movies that sort of dada-esque, fatal error happens. I was murmuring, "It's hopeless" into the ear of my weeping secretary (she is excessively sensitive) when the telephone rang. She answered, sniffling into her handkerchief, and turned to me:

"It's Paul Brett and he says it's urgent."

I picked up the receiver.

"Dorothy? You've heard the news?"

"No. At least I don't think so."

"My sweet . . . uh . . . Frank is dead."

I remained silent. He continued nervously.

"Frank Tyler. Your ex-husband. He killed himself last night."

"It's not true," I said.

I didn't believe it. Frank had never had an ounce of courage. Charming in every way, but no courage at all. And as I see it, it takes a lot of courage to kill yourself. Just think of all the people who have nothing better to do, and can't bring themselves to it.

"Yes," Paul continued. "He killed himself this morning in a third-rate motel. Not far from your place. No explanation."

My heart beat slowly, slowly. So hard and slowly. Frank . . . his gaiety, his laugh, his skin . . . Dead. Strange how the death of someone superficial shocks you more than the death of someone serious. I could not make myself believe it.

"Dorothy . . . do you hear me? . . ."

"I hear you."

"Dorothy, you must come. He had no family and you know Lola is in Rome. I'm sorry, Dorothy, but you've got to come and take care of the formalities. I'll stop by for you."

He hung up. I handed the phone to my secretary —she is called Candy, God knows why—and sat down. She looked at me and, with that second sense that makes her so precious, she got up, opened the drawer marked "Files," and handed me the opened bottle of Chivas Regal that is usually there. Absent-mindedly, I took a long swallow. I know why they give alcohol to people in shock: it's because alcohol is really disgusting and in such cases it awakens in one a sort of physical revulsion, a refusal, that brings you out of your torpor more easily than anything else. The whiskey burned my mouth and throat and I came to myself, horrified.

"Frank is dead," I said.

Candy returned to her handkerchief. Of course I had had lots of time, whenever I was without inspiration, to tell her the sad story of my life. She, too, for that matter. In short, she knew about Frank and that gave me a certain comfort. It would have been unsupportable at the moment when I learned of his death to be with someone who was unaware that he had existed. Yet, God knows, the poor thing had dropped out of sight a long time ago; he was all the more forgotten because he had been well known. The horrible thing about fame, here, is that when it does not last, it becomes something repulsive. By the simple line in the newspapers, by the vague remarks, nasty and almost without pity, that his suicide would cause,

Frank, who had been the handsome Frank, the envied husband of Lola Crevette, Frank, who had laughed with me, was going to die twice.

Paul arrived quickly. He took my arm in a friendly way, but made no move of sympathy, which—I knew—would have caused me to burst into tears. I have always kept an affection, a tenderness, for the men with whom I have slept, good or bad. Something quite rare, it seems. But at night, in bed, there comes a moment when you feel closer to the man who is with you than to anything else on earth, and no one can make me believe otherwise. Men's bodies, so valiant or so vulnerable, so different and so alike, so anxious, in fact, not to be alike . . . I took Paul's arm and we left. I was considerably relieved, too, never to have loved Paul. . . . In this recognition of the past that I was about to make, anyone really of the present would have been unbearable.

Frank lay there, asleep, indifferent, dead. He had fired a bullet directly into his heart at two inches, so his face was intact. I said good-by to him without too much trouble, as I imagine one says good-by to some part of oneself, something that has been oneself, and that a shell burst, an operation, or an accident takes from one. His hair had always been brown; strangely, I had never seen a man with such brown hair, and yet, it was an ordinary color. Paul decided to take me back to the house. I obeyed. It was four in the afternoon, the sun burned our faces in Paul's new

Jaguar, and I was thinking that it would never again burn Frank's face, he who had loved it so much. The dead are not treated very kindly: they are scarcely dead when they are shut up in dark boxes, tightly closed, and then into the ground. Get rid of them. Or they are made up, disfigured, displayed under pale electric lights, transformed into rigidity. It seems to me that they should be exposed to the sun for ten minutes, taken to the seashore, if they loved it; they should be offered the earth, in fact, one last time before they are joined with it forever. But no, they are punished for their death. At best, we play them a bit of Bach, or religious music that they usually did not like. I was weighed down with melancholy when Paul dropped me at my door.

"Would you like me to come in for a moment?"

I nodded mechanically, then I thought of Lewis. Oh well, it was of no importance! I was completely indifferent to their silent, icy stares, completely indifferent to what they thought of each other. So Paul followed me as far as the terrace, where Lewis, stretched out in his rocking chair, was watching the birds. He waved to me from a distance, but stopped abruptly when he saw Paul. I walked up the terrace steps and stood before him.

"Lewis," I said, "Frank is dead."

He stretched out his hand, touched my hair with a hesitant gesture, and suddenly I broke down. I fell to my knees at his feet and sobbed against this child who knew nothing of life's sorrows. His hand lightly brushed my hair, my forehead, my tear-streaked cheek; he said nothing. When I was calmer I looked up. Paul had left without a word. And suddenly I realized that I had not cried in front of him for a horrible and pitiful reason: it was what he had hoped for.

"I must be a sight to see," I said to Lewis.

I looked into his face. I knew my eyes were swollen, my mascara running, my features distorted. And for the first time in my life, in front of a man, it didn't bother me at all. In Lewis's look, in the moral reflection of myself that he returned to me, I saw only a child in tears—Dorothy Seymour, forty-five years old. There was something in him, something obscure, frightening, and reassuring all at the same time, something that denied false appearances.

"It's hard for you," he said dreamily.

"I loved him a long time."

"He left you, he's been punished," he said briefly. "That's life."

"You're childish. Life isn't as childish as you, thank God."

"It can be."

He was no longer looking at me; he had resumed his contemplation of the birds, his manner absent, almost bored. I thought for an instant that his sympathy did not go very far; I missed Brett's shoulder, the memories of Frank we could have called up, the way he would have dried my tears from time to time —in short, the frightful, tearful, sentimental comedy we could have played on this same terrace. Just the same, I was strangely proud to have abstained from it. I went into the house, the telephone rang. It did not stop ringing all evening. My former lovers, my friends, my poor secretary, Frank's partners, the reporters (not many, however), all hung on the telephone. They already knew that when Lola Crevette had heard the news in Rome she had taken the occasion to faint and leave the set, accompanied by her new Italian gigolo. I was vaguely sickened by all this ado. Not one of them, so sympathetic now, had ever helped Frank. And it was I, scorning the American divorce laws, who had supported him financially to the end. The last blow was given by Jerry Bolton, the head of Actors Associated. This person, repulsive if ever a person was, had filed suit after suit against me upon my return from Europe, had tried to reduce me to begging, and then, when that failed, had turned on Frank after Lola had left him. He was all-powerful, surly, truly a contemptible man, and he knew that I dearly hated him. He was insolent enough to call me.

"Dorothy? I'm so sorry. I know that you loved Frank deeply, and I . . ."

"I know that you threw him out, Jerry, and that

you practically had him blacklisted everywhere. Hang up, please, I hate being rude."

He hung up. My anger did me good. I went back into the living room and explained to Lewis all the reasons why I hated Jerry Bolton and his dollars and his omnipotence.

"If I hadn't had a few friends and steel nerves, he would have driven me to suicide as he did Frank. He's the most hypocritical bastard of them all. I've never wished for anyone's death, but I almost wish for his. He's the only person of whom I can say that."

With that my speech ended.

"That's because you're not demanding enough," said Lewis, absently. "There are surely others."

5

I was sitting in my office at RKB, fidgeting nervously, my eyes fixed on the telephone. Candy was pale with emotion. Only Lewis, sitting in the visitor's chair, seemed calm, almost bored. We waited together for the results of his screen test.

He had suddenly decided, one evening, several days after Frank's death. He stood up, took three steps very straight, easily, as though he had never been injured, and stopped in front of me.

"Look, I'm well again."

I realized suddenly that I had become so used to his presence, his physical handicap, that I had never imagined this, and now it had happened. He would tell me, "Good-by, thank you," and leave the house; I would not see him again. A strange sadness came over me.

"That's good news," I said feebly.

"Do you think so?"

"Of course. What . . . what are you going to do now?"

"That depends on you," he said calmly, and sat down again.

I caught my breath. At least he was not leaving immediately. At the same time, what he had said intrigued me. How could the destiny of someone so volatile, so indifferent, so free as he was, depend upon me? Actually I had never been more than a sort of nurse to him.

"If I stay here I'll have to work, in any case," he continued.

"Are you thinking of settling down in Los Angeles?"

"I said 'here,' " he said sternly, motioning toward the terrace and his chair. Then he added, after a moment, "If that doesn't bother you, of course."

I dropped my cigarette, picked it up again, and stood up, mumbling something like, "Well, tell me . . . ah . . . I see . . . really, if I'd expected . . ." and so on. He looked at me without moving. Horribly ill at ease, which was really the limit, I hurried to the kitchen and took a long drink from the bottle of whiskey. I would end up an alcoholic if I wasn't one already. Somewhat steadied, I returned to the terrace. It was time for me to explain to this boy that I lived alone by choice, by my own decision, and that I was not in need of a young man's company. And that, besides, his being here would keep me from bringing my suitors to the house, which was a terrible nuisance. And besides, besides, besides . . . In short, that there was no reason for him to stay. Suddenly I was as indignant about his decision to stay as I had been sad two minutes before when I thought of his leaving. But my contradictions no longer surprised me.

"Lewis," I said, "it's time we had a little talk."

"There's no need," he said. "If you don't want me to stay, I'll leave."

"It's not that," I said, caught off guard.

"What else is there?"

I looked at him, stunned. Yes, what else was there? But it was not only that. I did not want him to leave. I liked him very much.

"It's not proper," I said feebly.

He burst into laughter, the laughter that made him seem so young. I became angry.

"As long as you were sick, injured, it was normal for me to keep you here. You were in the street, sick, you . . ."

"So, now I'm walking again, it's no longer proper?"

"Now there's no explanation."

"Now there's no explanation for whom?"

"For everyone!"

"Do you explain your way of life to everyone?"

The contempt in his tone of voice exasperated me.

"Really, Lewis, what do you think? I have my life, friends—I even, er . . . there are even men who are interested in me."

With the last remark, the total humiliation, I felt myself blushing. At forty-five! Lewis nodded.

"I know very well there are men in love with you. That fellow Brett, for instance."

"There's never been anything between Paul and me," I said virtuously. "And besides, that's not your affair. Just understand that your being here is compromising for me."

"You're a big girl now," said Lewis, rightly enough. "I only thought that if I worked in the city, I could go on living here, and I could pay you board."

"But I don't need money. I earn my living without taking in lodgers."

"I'd feel better about it," Lewis said calmly.

After an endless discussion, we reached a compromise. Lewis would look for a job, and after a while he would hunt for somewhere else to live—in the neighborhood, if he insisted. He accepted these conditions. We retired in perfect agreement. The only question we had not touched upon, I realized before going to sleep, was simply this: why did he want to stay with me?

The next day I made the rounds of the studios, spoke of a marvelously good-looking young man, and collected several acid remarks and an appointment for Lewis. He went to the studio with me, calmly took his screen test, and Jay Grant, my boss, promised to see him one day the following week. . . .

That was today. Jay was in the projection room viewing the tests of Lewis and a dozen other young hopefuls; I chewed on my pen, and Candy, who had fallen in love with Lewis at first sight, was typing without interest at her desk.

"You don't have much of a view," Lewis said idly.

I looked out the window at the yellow lawn below. That was the important thing! He might become a great star, the USA's seducer number ONE, and he talked about my view! Suddenly I imagined him as the idol of the masses, loaded down with Oscars, pushing through the crowd, and from time to time making a little detour in his Cadillac to say hello to poor old Dorothy, who was the one responsible for it all. I was beginning to feel pleased with myself when the telephone rang. My hand was moist when I picked up the receiver.

"Dorothy? This is Jay. Honey, your little friend is very good, he's superb. Come and look at the test. He's the best I've seen since James Dean."

"He's here," I said in a strangled voice.

"Fine. Bring him along."

After Candy had embraced us, wiping her eyes again, we jumped into my car, broke all speed records for the two miles that separated us from the studio, and we fell into Jay's arms. I say "we" loosely, because Lewis whistled, dragged his feet, and appeared to be completely bored by the whole business. He greeted Jay politely, sat down in the dark next to me, and they ran his screen test.

He had a different face on the screen, something indefinable, violent, cruel, extremely attractive, I must admit, but something that made me feel uneasy. It was an unknown who, with an incredible offhandedness and presence, got up, leaned against a wall, lit a cigarette, yawned, smiled, as though he were all alone. One could see that the camera had not bothered him; it almost seemed that he was unaware of it. The lights went on and Jay turned to me, triumphant.

"Well, Dorothy, what do you think?"

He was the one who had made the discovery, naturally. I nodded several times, without saying anything, the sort of mimicry that works best here. Jay turned to Lewis.

"What do you think of yourself?"

"I don't think of myself," Lewis said soberly.

"Where did you learn to act?"

"Nowhere."

"Nowhere? Come, come, my friend . . ."

Lewis stood up. He suddenly seemed disgusted.
"I never lie, Mr. uh . . . uh . . ."

"Grant," Jay said mechanically.

"I never lie, Mr. Grant."

For the first time in my life I saw Jay Grant undone. He blushed slightly.

"I didn't say that you lied. I simply said that you were surprisingly natural for a beginner. Dorothy can tell you."

He turned toward me, and his pleading look made me want to laugh. I went to his aid.

"It's true, Lewis, you're very good."

He looked at me, smiled, and suddenly leaned toward me, as though we were alone.

"Really? You liked me?"

His face was an inch from mine. I squirmed in my chair, terribly uneasy.

"Yes, Lewis, I'm sure you have a career before you. I . . ."

Jay coughed discreetly, as I had thought he would.

"I'll prepare your contract, Lewis, and you can show it to your lawyer if you like. How can I reach you?"

Buried in my armchair, stunned, I heard Lewis reply calmly, "I'm living at Mrs. Seymour's."

6

The scandal was small, because of my slight importance in Hollywood. A few remarks here and there, several stupid congratulations on the successful future of "my protégé." But the rumor went no further than my office. No columnist knocked at the door. A simple line in a trade paper announced that a young unknown, Lewis Miles, had been signed by the famous Jay Grant. Paul Brett was the only one who, seriously, during an impromptu lunch at the studio commissary, asked me what I was going to do with Lewis. Paul had lost weight, which became him, and he had the sad manner so common among men in their forties in this country. And suddenly he made me remember that men and love existed. I gaily replied that I was not concerned with Lewis, that I was happy for him, and that he would be moving out soon. He looked at me suspiciously.

"Dorothy, I've always liked you because you don't lie and because you don't play idiotic comedies like the other women here."

"So?"

"Don't tell me that you've been living innocently for a month with a handsome young man. I'll admit that he's handsome. . . ."

I began to laugh.

"Paul, you must believe me. He doesn't interest me, not in that way. Any more than I interest him. I know it seems strange, but that's how it is."

"Will you swear to that?"

Charming, the mania that men have for swearing to things. So I swore that it was true and, to my surprise, Paul's face literally lit up. To my surprise, because I had not thought he was so gullible as to believe in a woman's promise, no matter what it was, or that he was so infatuated with me that my promise would please him. I realized that, in fact, I had been living for over a month with Lewis, that I had scarcely gone out during that time, and yet, that I had not been ensconced in the depths of a large bed with a good-looking man, though that was something that had always been important in my life. I studied Paul more attentively; I found charm, elegance, perfect manners, and I made a date with him for the following day. He would call for me around nine o'clock, we would have dinner at Chasen's and then go dancing. He left me, I left him, enchanted with each other.

The next day I came home earlier than usual, determined to dress sumptuously and seduce Paul Brett once and for all. Lewis was sitting in his chair, looking up at the sky as usual. He limply waved a paper in front of me. I took it as I passed. It was the contract with Grant. It provided for three films with Lewis, a perfectly honest weekly salary for two years, and, naturally, exclusive rights. I scanned it quickly and recommended that he show it to my lawyer to be certain.

"Are you happy, Lewis?"

"It's all the same to me," he said. "If it looks good to you, I'll sign. You're in a hurry?"

"I have a dinner date," I said cheerfully. "Paul Brett is coming to pick me up in an hour."

I went up the stairs, jumped into the bathtub, and once settled in the hot water, thought of my future with great optimism. Decidedly, I managed to get out of the most complicated situations: Lewis was going to have a brilliant career, Paul still loved me, we were going to have dinner, amuse ourselves, perhaps make love, life was wonderful. I looked in the mirror at my still slender body, my radiant expression, and I was humming as I slipped into the beautiful Porthault bathrobe that my daughter had sent me from Paris. I settled myself at the dressing table, got out my numerous jars of magic creams, and began the operation. It was in the mirror that I saw Lewis enter. He came into the bedroom without knocking—a thing that surprised me without upsetting me much because, as I said, I was in perfect humor—and he sat down on the floor beside me. I had done one eye and not the other, which gave me a rather stupid look, and I quickly attacked the problem.

"Where are you going to have dinner?" asked Lewis.

"Chasen's. It's in Los Angeles, the one restaurant where you have to have been. Soon you'll be going there as a star."

"Don't talk nonsense."

His voice was curt, nasty. I stopped a moment, the eyebrow pencil in my hand poised in the air.

"I'm not talking nonsense. It's a charming place."

He did not answer. He looked out the window as usual. I finished my make-up and, strangely, hesitated to put on my lipstick in front of him. It seemed indecent, like undressing in front of a child. I went into the bathroom, carefully traced a mouth à la Crawford, and put on a midnight blue dress, a Saint-Laurent copy, the one I preferred. I had a problem with the zipper which made me completely forget Lewis as I came out, and I almost stumbled over him, still sitting on the carpet. He jumped up and glared at me. I smiled at him, proud of myself.

"What do you think of me?" I asked.

"I like you better as a gardener," he said.

I laughed and headed for the door. It was time that I prepared the cocktails. But Lewis caught me by the arm.

"And me, what am I going to do?"

"Do as you please," I said, astonished. "There's television, smoked salmon in the refrigerator . . . or if you want to take my car, you can. . . ."

He still held me by the arm, his expression firm and at the same time undecided. He looked at me blankly and I recognized the blind look that had so impressed me at the studio: the look of a stranger on earth. I tried to free my arm, but did not succeed, and suddenly I hoped that Paul would arrive quickly.

"Let go of me, Lewis, I'm late."

I spoke softly, as though not to awaken him. I saw the perspiration on his forehead, around his mouth. I wondered if he was sick. At that instant he saw me, snapped out of it, let go of my arm.

"Your necklace is badly fastened," he said.

He put his hands around my neck and, with great ease, attached the safety clasp on my pearls. Then he stepped back and I left the room. It had only lasted a second, but I, too, felt a tiny drop of water run down the nape of my neck, down my back. And that had nothing to do with the physical agitation that the contact of a man's hand on your neck can make. I knew that agitation well and it was not the same.

Paul arrived on time, was charming with Lewis—slightly condescending but charming—and the three of us had a cocktail. My optimism returned quickly. As I left, I waved to Lewis, motionless in the doorway, a long, slim silhouette, handsome, so handsome—too handsome. The evening passed as I had expected, I saw a thousand friends, I danced two hours with Paul, and he was a bit high when he took me to his apartment. I found again the pleasure of the smell of tobacco, the weight of a man, and the loving words whispered in the dark. Paul was virile, tender, told me he loved me, and asked me to marry him. I accepted, naturally, pleasure having always made me say yes, no matter what. At six in the morning, I forced him to take me home; Lewis's window was closed and only the morning wind rustled the tall weeds in my garden.

7

A month passed. Lewis had begun to work—a supporting role in a sentimental Western in color. Nevertheless, when they showed the rushes in the evening, he so dominated the screen that people were starting to talk about him. He seemed not to care. He walked about the studio, not saying a word, or passed as much time as possible in my office, flattered by Candy, or daydreamed among the old Hollywood sets, especially those for the B Westerns, those that are never dismantled, whole villages, with balconies and wooden stairways, false fronts with nothing behind them, hollow, touching, and morbid at the same time. Lewis walked for hours in these false streets, would sit down in a stairway, smoke a cigarette. In the evening I took him back to the house. I often left him alone. Alone in spite of my suggestions. Paul was determined to drag me before the preacher, and it took all of my diplomacy to resist him. Everyone thought I was sharing the charms of two men, playing the siren, which made me feel young but was annoying.

This marvelous situation lasted nearly three weeks. How could I ever say how wonderful life is when you love it? The beautiful days, the agitation of the nights, the dizziness from alcohol and from pleasure, the violins of tenderness, the excitement of working, the unbelievable happiness of waking up alive, with so much time before you, an entire gigantic day before sleep stills you again in a mortal pose, on the pillow. I can never be thankful enough to heaven, or God, or my mother, for having put me on earth. Everything was mine: the freshness of the sheets or their clamminess, my lover's shoulder close to me or my solitude, the gray and blue ocean, the smooth, slick road that led to the studio, the music on the radio, and Lewis's imploring look.

That was the stumbling block. I was beginning to feel guilty. Each night I had the feeling that I was abandoning him. When I drove to the set where he was working, when I shut the car door and headed toward him with, I hoped, the harmonious stride of a well-balanced woman, I saw that he was contracted, nervous, pensive, and I sometimes asked myself, in a sort of delirium, if I was not fooling myself . . . if this life, mine, the happiness at being alive, the gaiety, the love, the sense of accomplishment, was not just a stupid trap . . . if I should not run to him, take him in my arms, and ask him . . . ask him what? . . . Something frightened me. I felt that I was being drawn toward something unknown, morbid, but distinctly "real." Then I would pull myself together, laugh, and say, "Hello, Lewis," and he would return my smile. Once or twice I saw him in action. He was as still as an animal before the greedy camera, making few gestures, and so absent in manner that he became as implacable as the lions, weary of the zoo, that you cannot look in the eye.

Then Bolton decided to buy him. For him it was easy. There was not a producer in Hollywood in a position to refuse him anything, Jay Grant included. He made an appointment with Lewis, offered him better terms, and bought his contract with Jay. I was furious. Especially because Lewis refused to talk about their meeting. I was forced to pester him.

"It's a big desk. He was behind it with a cigarette. He asked me to sit down, then picked up the phone and called some other guy."

"What did you do then?"

"There was a magazine lying on his desk; I started to read."

At that point, I began to be amused. A young man

reading a magazine in front of Bolton was delightful to imagine.

"And then?"

"When he had hung up, he asked me if I thought I was at the dentist's."

"What did you answer?"

"No. That I had never been to the dentist, anyway. I have very, very good teeth."

He leaned toward me and raised his upper lip with his finger to prove that what he had said was true. His teeth were white and pointed, like those of a wolf. I nodded in agreement.

"And then?"

"And then, nothing. He mumbled something and told me that I should be honored by his interest in me or something like that. That he was going to buy my contract, that he would make me a career, uh . . . how did he put it? . . . an impressive career."

Suddenly he began to laugh.

"Impressive . . . me! . . . I told him I didn't care, that I only wanted to earn a lot of money. You know, I found a Rolls."

"A what?"

"You know, a Rolls, like you were talking about with Paul the other day. The kind that you can get into without stooping. I've found one for you. It's forty years old, but it's very high and covered with gold on the inside. We'll have it next week. He gave me enough money for the down payment, so I signed."

I was stunned for a moment.

"Are you telling me that you've bought me a Rolls?"

"Didn't you want one?"

"And you think you're going to make all my schoolgirl dreams come true like that? Are you mad?"

He made a tender, appeasing gesture that seemed a bit old for him. Our roles were reversed. Our situation, even though it was platonic, had become comic. Touching, but comic. He must have seen it on my face because he became gloomy.

"I thought it would please you," he said. "Excuse me, I have to go out tonight."

Before I could say a word, he got up and left the terrace. I went to bed, full of regrets, got up again about midnight to write him a thank-you letter, with excuses so sugary that I was finally obliged to cross out some of the expressions. I slipped the letter under his pillow and stayed awake a long time waiting for him. But at four in the morning he had still not arrived and I concluded with a mixture of relief and sadness that he had found a mistress at last.

Because I had slept badly I had taken the receiver off the telephone and I was ignorant of what had happened when, still yawning, I arrived at my office about noon. Candy jumped up from her chair, her eyes dark and nervous. One might have thought that her electric typewriter was plugged into her tibia. She threw her arms around my neck.

"What do you think of it, Dorothy? What do you think?"

"Of what, my God?"

I had a horrible vision of a new contract with even more money. I was in the middle of a lazy period, but she would not let me refuse it. In spite of the fact that I was obviously healthy, ever since my childhood everyone had watched over me as though I were mentally retarded.

"You don't know?"

The pleasure in her expression doubled.

"Jerry Bolton is dead."

I must admit, with horror, that like her, and like everyone else in the company for that matter, I took this as good news. I sat down in front of her and noticed that she had already taken out the bottle of scotch and two glasses, as though to celebrate.

"What do you mean, dead? Lewis saw him only yesterday afternoon."

"Murdered."

She was in high heaven. I asked myself if my verbose literary creations were not somehow responsible for her melodramatic manner.

"But by whom?"

She suddenly became embarrassed and prudish.

"I don't know if I can tell you. . . . It seems that Mr. Bolton had . . . er . . . morals . . . that . . . . that . . ."

"Candy," I said sternly, "everyone has morals, no matter what they are. Explain yourself."

"They found him in a 'special' house, near Malibu, where he was an old client, it seems. He had entered with a young man that they haven't found, who killed him. The radio called it a vile crime."

Jerry Bolton had hidden his game well for thirty years. For thirty years he had played the role of the unconsolable, straitlaced widower. For thirty years he had smeared mud on certain effeminate young actors, often ruining their careers, and all this, no doubt, in self-defense. . . . It was absurd.

"Why didn't they stifle the affair?"

"The murderer, they think, called the police right afterward, and then the newspapers. They discovered the body at midnight. It was too late to do anything about it. The owner of the place had to put his cards on the table."

I picked up the glass on the desk mechanically, then, disgusted, put it back. It was a bit early to start drinking. I decided to make a round of the offices. They were lively. I might even say that they were hilarious, which bothered me a little. A man's death, finally, could never make me happy. All these people had at some time or other been humiliated or ruined by Bolton, and the double news of his secret life and of his death gave them a morbid pleasure. I left quickly and went to the set where Lewis was acting. He had started to work at eight o'clock, and after the night he had spent he could not be in very good condition. Nevertheless, I found him leaning against a piece of scenery, smiling and at ease. He came toward me.

"Lewis . . . have you heard the news?"

"Yes. Of course. We're not shooting tomorrow, as a sign of mourning. We can do some gardening."

After a pause, he added, "I can't say that I brought him luck."

"It's not too good for your career."

He dismissed the subject with a relaxed wave of his hand.

"Did you find my letter, Lewis?"

He looked at me and began to blush.

"No. I stayed out all night."

I burst into laughter.

"You have every right. I only wanted to tell you that I was happy about the Rolls, that I was so surprised that I couldn't make you understand, that's all. I was sorry afterward."

"You should never feel sorry because of me," he said. "Never."

They called him. He had a short love scene with a starlet, June Power, an open-mouthed brunette. She settled herself in his arms with evident enthusiasm and I felt that Lewis, from now on, would not be spending his nights at the house. After all, it was normal, and I left for the studio commissary, where I was going to have lunch with Paul.

8

The Rolls was an enormous and curious object: a touring car, a dirty white, with black cushions—or what should have been black—and gleaming bits of copper everywhere. It must have been a 1925 model, at best. A real horror. As there was only space for one car in my garage, we were obliged to park it in the garden, which was already overcrowded. A few tall weeds poked up on both sides in a charming way. Lewis was enchanted, walked around the auto, and even deserted his chair on the terrace in favor of the back seat. Little by little he filled it with his books, cigarettes, and bottles, and as soon as he returned from the studio he would settle down there, his feet sticking over the side of the car, filling his lungs with a mixture of the smell of night and the musty smell that emanated from the old cushions. Thank God he said nothing about putting it in running order; that was the main thing. I had no idea, in fact, how it had managed to get as far as the house.

We decided, by mutual agreement, to wash it every Sunday. Anyone who has not cleaned, on a Sunday morning, a 1925 Rolls, installed like a statue in a run-down garden, has missed one of life's greatest joys. It took us an hour and a half for the outside, a half-hour for the inside. I would begin by helping Lewis, taking charge of the headlights and the grille. Then I would go at the cushions alone. The interior was my realm, and I became a housekeeper such as I had never been in my own home. I put a special wax on the cushions, then polished them with a chamois. I wiped the wood on the dashboard, made it shine. Then I cleaned the dials with my breath, and my delighted eyes saw the 80-mile-per-hour figure in the shining speedometer. Outside, Lewis, in a T-shirt, went at the tires, spokes, and bumpers. At half-past twelve the Rolls was sparkling, magnificent, and we were wildly happy; we walked around it as we drank our cocktails, congratulating ourselves on the morning's work. I know why: it had been completely useless. The week would pass. The brambles would creep up over the car, and we would never make use of it. But we would begin again the next Sunday. Together we would rediscover the pleasures of childhood: the most frantic, most gratuitous, most profound. The following day, Monday, we would return to our paid labors, precise and regular, that allowed us to eat, drink, and sleep, the labors which would reassure "others" about our life. But God, how I sometimes hated life and its workings. It's strange: perhaps one must hate life deep down, as I always had, in order to love it in all its aspects.

One lovely evening in September I was lying on the terrace, snuggled in one of Lewis's sweaters, heavy, coarse, and warm, as I like them. I had persuaded him, with some difficulty, to follow me into a shop, and he had, thanks to his brilliant salary, replenished a non-existent wardrobe. I often borrowed his sweaters; I have always done that with those with whom I've lived—one of the only vices, I think, with which they can justly reproach me. I drowsed, at the same time reading an especially fatuous synopsis for which I was to write the dialogue in three weeks' time. It concerned, I think, a stupid young girl who encounters an intelligent young man and comes into bloom as a result of the meeting, or something of that sort. The only problem was that the stupid young girl seemed to me to be more intelligent than the young man. In any case, it was a best-seller, and the story line could not be changed. So I yawned and eagerly hoped for Lewis's arrival. But what did I see arrive instead, in a poor little tweed suit, almost black, but with an enormous brooch at the collar: the famous, the ideal Lola Crevette, home from Cinecitta.

She stopped in front of my humble dwelling, murmured a few words to her chauffeur, and pushed open my gate. She had some trouble in getting around the Rolls, and there was stupor in her black eyes when she saw me. I must have looked most peculiar with my hair hanging over my eyes, wrapped in that enormous sweater, nestled in a rattan chaise longue, a bottle of scotch beside me. I must have looked like one of those alcoholic and solitary Tennessee Williams heroines that I like so much. Lola stopped at the foot of the three steps to the terrace, and in a broken voice pronounced my name: "Dorothy, Dorothy . . ." I looked at her, amazed. Lola Crevette was a national institution; she never went anywhere without a bodyguard, a lover, and fifteen photographers. What was she doing in my garden? We stared at each other like two owls, and I could not help thinking that she took wonderful care of herself. At forty-three she had the beauty, the skin, the éclat of a twenty-year-old. She said again, "Dorothy . . ." and I feebly got up from the chair and croaked, "Lola . . ." in a tone as colorless as it was polite. Then she hurried, jumping up the steps like a young deer, an exertion that made her breasts shake pitifully under the suit. She fell into my arms. I realized at that moment that we were, both of us, Frank's widows.

"My God, Dorothy, when I think that I wasn't here . . . that you had to take care of everything all alone. . . . Yes, I know . . . you've been marvelous; everyone says so. . . . I had to come to see you . . . I had to. . . ."

She had paid no attention to Frank for five years; she had not even seen him. So I imagined that she had a free afternoon, or that her new lover was unable to satisfy her emotional requirements. There is nothing like a bored woman to go looking for sorrow. Philosophically, I offered her a chair, a drink, and we began the concert in praise of Frank. She began by excusing herself for having taken him from me (but passion excuses everything), I began by pardoning her (but time arranges everything), and we went on from there. Actually, she amused me somewhat. She spoke in clichés, with perfectly terrifying little moments of candor, of ferocity. We were reminiscing about the summer of 1959 when Lewis arrived.

He jumped over the bumper of the Rolls, smiling. He was slim and handsome as few men are. He wore an old jacket and cotton slacks, his black hair falling over his eyes. I saw that as I saw it every day, but I saw it especially in Lola's look. It seems strange to say: she faltered. She faltered as a horse does before an obstacle, as a woman can before a man she desires too much and too quickly. Lewis's smile vanished when he saw her; he detested strangers. I introduced them amicably and Lola got out her weapons immediately.

She was not a fool or a part-time coquette; she was a woman with a head on her shoulders, a woman with status, a professional. I admired her act myself. She did not try for a second to dazzle Lewis, or even excite him. She took on the style of the house, spoke of the car, nonchalantly served herself another drink, absently asked about Lewis's projects—in short, played the friendly woman, easy to get along with, and far removed from all that (meaning Hollywood). By the look she gave me, I saw at once that she assumed Lewis was my lover and had decided to take him away from me. That would be a bit much, after poor Frank, but then . . . I was slightly irritated, I admit. It was one thing for her to amuse herself with Lewis, but for her to make a fool of me, to carry it that far . . . It's frightening what blunders vanity can cause. For the first time in six months I made a possessive gesture toward Lewis. He was sitting on the ground watching us, without saying much. I held out my hand to him.

"Lean against my chair, Lewis; you'll give yourself a backache."

He leaned against my chair and I ran my hand casually through his hair. He immediately threw back his head, against my knees, with a sudden violence. He had shut his eyes; he smiled, he seemed to be perfectly happy, and I withdrew my hand from his hair as though I had been burned. Lola had become pale, but that did not give me the slightest pleasure: I was ashamed of myself.

Even so, Lola continued the conversation for a while, with a cold-bloodedness that was all the more noteworthy because Lewis had not moved his head from my knees and appeared to be not at all interested in the conversation. We surely gave the impression of having the perfect love affair, and when the first uneasiness had passed, I felt a fit of laughter coming on. Lola finally wearied and got up. I did the same, which visibly disturbed Lewis: he stood up and stretched, staring at Lola with a look so icy, so bored, so impatient for her to leave that she returned his stare, coldly, as though she were looking at an inanimate object.

"I'll leave you, Dorothy. I'm afraid I've disturbed you. I'm leaving you in good-looking company, even if it's not good."

Lewis did not budge. Nor I. Her chauffeur had already opened the car door. Lola bristled.

"Don't you know, young man, that ladies are usually accompanied to the door?"

She had turned toward Lewis, and stunned, I heard her, for one of the few times in her life, lose her famous self-control.

"Ladies, yes," said Lewis calmly. And he did not move.

Lola raised her hand as if to slap him, and I shut my eyes. Lola was as well known for her slaps in real life as on the screen. She did it very well in either case, first with the palm, then with the back of the hand, without the slightest movement of her shoulders. But now she stopped short. Then I, too, looked at Lewis. He was still, blind, deaf, as I had seen him once before; he was breathing slowly and he had the same tiny beads of perspiration around his mouth. Lola took a step backward, then two, as if to get out of his reach. She was afraid and so was I.

"Lewis," I said. And I laid my hand on his arm. He came to life, bowed toward her, in a completely outmoded fashion. She glared at us.

"You should find them less young, Dorothy, and more polite."

I did not reply. I was leveled. All Hollywood would know about it tomorrow. And Lola would take her revenge. That meant two weeks of constant torment.

Lola gone, I could not help but make a few remarks to Lewis. He looked at me with pity in his eyes.

"Does that really bother you?"

"Yes, I hate gossips."

"I'll take care of that," he said peaceably.

But he did not have the time. The following morning, on her way to the studio, Lola Crevette's convertible missed a curve and she crashed into the valley, a hundred yards below.

 67

9

The funeral was sumptuous. In two months' time, with Jerry Bolton, that made two Hollywood celebrities who had died tragically. Countless wreaths from countless survivors covered the cemetery. I was with Paul and Lewis. For me, it was the third time. After Frank it had been Bolton. Once again I strode down the neatly trimmed paths. I had buried three persons, so different, but all of them at the same time weak and ruthless, avid and disillusioned, three persons driven by a frenzy as mysterious for themselves as it was for others. It was most depressing, when one thought about it. What is it in life that always stands between people and their most intimate desires, their frightful determination to be happy? Is it the image of that happiness that they form and then can never reconcile with their lives? Is it time or the absence of time? Is it a nostalgia nurtured from infancy?

Back at the house, sitting between my two men, I talked about this at some length, laboriously questioning them and the stars. Neither seemed capable of answering me. I can even say that the stars winked as feebly at my discourse as the eyes of my two companions. Yet I had put *La Traviata* on the record player, music as romantic as it can be, and which has always inclined me to meditation. I finally had had enough of their silence.

"Well, Lewis, you, are you happy?"

"Yes."

His terse reply should have discouraged me. I persisted.

"And do you know why?"

"No."

I turned to Paul.

"And you, Paul?"

"I hope to be completely happy very soon."

This allusion to our marriage slightly chilled my blood. I dodged it quickly.

"But look. The three of us are here, it's warm, the earth is round, we're in good health, we're happy. . . . Why does everyone we know have that hungry, hunted look? . . . What's happening?"

"For pity's sake, Dorothy," groaned Paul, "I don't know. Read the newspapers, they're full of articles on the subject."

"Why doesn't anyone ever want to speak seriously with me?" I said, furious. "Am I a goose? Am I completely stupid?"

"One can't talk seriously about happiness with you," said Paul. "You're a living answer. I couldn't discuss God's existence with God himself."

"It's because," said Lewis abruptly, almost stuttering, "it's because you're good."

He stood up suddenly, and the light from the living room fell upon him. He looked strange, his hand raised like a prophet's.

"You . . . you understand . . . you're good. People generally aren't good at all, so . . . so they can't even be good with themselves, and . . ."

"My God," said Paul, "why don't we have another drink? Somewhere a little gayer? . . . Will you come along, Lewis?"

It was the first time that he had invited him and, to my great surprise, Lewis accepted. We decided to go to one of the hippie clubs near Malibu. The three of us crowded into Paul's Jaguar and I laughingly observed that Lewis was better there than the first time we had encountered him in front of the car. After that clever remark we headed down the road, top down, the wind in our eyes and our ears. I felt marvelously well, squeezed between my lover and my

little brother, almost my son, two handsome, gener-
ous, kind men whom I loved. I thought of poor Lola,
dead and buried, and thought how unbelievably
lucky I was, and that life was a marvelous gift.

The club in question was crammed with young
people, most of them sporting beards and long hair,
and we had a hard time finding a table. If Paul really
wanted to escape my conversation, he had succeeded:
the music was so violent you could not say a word.
Nevertheless, a happy crowd jumped and jerked
about and the scotch was drinkable. At first I did not
notice Lewis's absence. It was only when he returned
to sit down at the table that I noticed his slightly
glassy-eyed expression, and I was surprised: he never
drank very much. Taking advantage of a slow piece, I
danced awhile with Paul, and I was returning to the
table when the accident happened.

A perspiring, bearded fellow crossed my path and
bumped into me, near the table. I murmured, "Par-
don me," mechanically, but he turned and stared at
me with a look so surly that it frightened me. He
must have been about eighteen, with a motorcycle on
the outside and several drinks too many on the inside.
He looked like one of those infamous leather-jackets
the magazines were going on about at the time. He
literally barked at me:

"What are you doing here, old lady?"

I had a second's time to become angry, and I did.
The human projectile that shot past me the next

second, and jumped at his throat, was Lewis. They rolled on the floor in the midst of tipped-over tables and the dancers' feet. The din was frightening. I called piercingly for Paul and saw that he was trying to cut his way through the mob a yard away. But the young crowd, delighted, formed a circle around the combatants and blocked his passage. I cried, "Lewis, Lewis," but he rolled on the floor, with muffled groans, still grasping leather-jacket by the throat. That lasted for a minute, a full minute of nightmare. Suddenly the two of them stopped and rested motionless on the floor. You could not see them clearly in the dark, but that stillness was even more frightening than their blows. Suddenly someone shouted:

"Separate them, separate them!"

Paul had come up beside me. He pushed aside the front-row spectators, if I may call them that, and hurtled forward. Then I distinctly saw Lewis's hand. That long, thin hand, clutching a boy's throat, squeezing frantically. I saw Paul's hand seize that hand, bend back the fingers, one by one, then I was shoved and fell, stunned, into a chair.

The rest was confused: they were holding Lewis in one corner and reviving leather-jacket in the other. As it was obvious that nobody wanted to call the police, we left quickly, the three of us, panting and in disarray. Lewis seemed calmed, calmed and distant. We climbed into the Jaguar without saying a word. Paul breathed heavily, took a cigarette, lit it, and handed it to me. Then he lit one for himself. He did not start the car.

I turned toward him and in as gay a voice as possible said, "Well, well . . . what an evening. . . ."

He did not answer but leaned across me and looked quizzically at Lewis.

"What have you taken, Lewis? LSD?"

Lewis did not reply. I sat up suddenly and looked at him. His head was thrown back, he stared at the sky, in another world.

"That doesn't change the fact," continued Paul softly, "that you almost killed someone. . . . What happened, Dorothy?"

I hesitated. It was not easy to say.

"The boy insinuated that I was a bit . . . er . . . old for the club."

I hoped Paul would cry out or be indignant, but he only shrugged his shoulders and we slowly drove off.

We did not exchange a word until we reached the house. Lewis seemed to be sleeping, and I had the slightly revolting thought that he was, in fact, probably full of his precious LSD. For that matter, I have nothing against drugs: it's just that alcohol is sufficient and the rest frightens me. I am also afraid of airplanes, scuba diving, and psychiatry. The earth is the only thing that reassures me, however much mud there is in it. Once we had arrived, Lewis got out first, mumbled something, and disappeared into the house. Paul helped me climb out of the Jaguar and followed me to the terrace.

"Dorothy . . . do you remember what I told you about Lewis the first time?"

"Yes, Paul. But you like him now. Don't you?"

"Yes. Exactly. I . . ."

He stammered a little. Something rare for him. He took my hand, turned it over, kissed it.

"He . . . you know, I don't think he's completely normal. He really just missed killing that guy."

"Nobody can be normal with a lump of sugar drenched with their hateful stuff," I said, with logic.

"That doesn't alter the fact that he's violent and that I don't like the idea of your living with him."

"Sincerely, I think he's deeply fond of me and would never harm me."

"Anyway, he's slated to be a star and you'll soon be rid of him. Grant spoke to me of it. They're basing their next campaign on him. What's more, he has talent. . . . Dorothy, when are you going to marry me?"

"Soon," I said, "very soon."

I leaned toward him and kissed him lightly on the mouth. He sighed. I left him and went into the house to see what had become of the super-star of tomorrow. He was stretched out on the floor, on my Mexican rug, his head in his hands. I went to the kitchen, reheated the coffee, and filled a cup for Lewis, at the same time rehearsing *in petto* a discourse on the evils of drugs. Then I returned to the living room, knelt down next to him, and tapped him firmly on the shoulder. In vain.

"Lewis, drink this coffee."

He still did not move. I shook him. He was probably battling with a horde of Chinese dragons and multicolored serpents. That annoyed me a little but at the same time I thought of his fighting for me an hour before, and that makes any woman indulgent.

"Lewis, my darling," I murmured.

He turned over and threw himself into my arms. He shook with a strange sobbing, a violent sobbing that almost strangled him and that frightened me. He had buried his head on my shoulder, my precious coffee was spilled all over the carpet, and motionless, at once touched and terrified, I listened to the bizarre litany that escaped his lips, into my hair.

"I could have killed him. . . . Oh! I should have . . . in another second. . . . To say that . . . to you. . . . Ah! I had him. . . . I had him. . . ."

"But look, Lewis, you can't fight like that with people, it doesn't make sense."

"A pig . . . he was a pig . . . the eyes of a beast. They all have the eyes of a beast . . . all of them . . . you don't see. . . . They'll separate me from you and they'll get you, too . . . you . . . you, Dorothy."

I touched the back of his neck, caressed his hair,

kissed his temples; I was saddened as though before a child's sorrow. I murmured vague words of the sort: "Come on, calm down, see, it's nothing." Half kneeling like that, with a man's weight on my shoulder, I began to have a slight cramp in my calf, and said to myself that this sort of scene was not for a woman my age. It would have taken a pure young girl to restore his confidence and taste for life. I knew well how life could be, I knew too well. Finally he grew calmer. I let him slowly slide down my body and stretch out on the rug. I put my afghan over him and went upstairs to bed, exhausted.

10

I awoke in the middle of the night, shivering from an atrocious thought. I remained sitting in my bed, like an owl, in the dark, for almost an hour, fitting the pieces together. Then I went downstairs, still trembling, into the kitchen, made a cup of coffee, and on reflection, added a jigger of cognac. The dawn came. I walked onto the terrace, looked at the eastern sky, where a long line of white, already turning blue, was stretching out, then I looked at the Rolls, once again attacked by the brambles—it was Friday—then at Lewis's favorite chair, then at my hands gripping the terrace rail, but still trembling. I have no idea how long I remained like that, holding onto that rail. From time to time I tried to sit down in a chair but the same idea brought me to my feet immediately, like a puppet. I did not even smoke a cigarette.

At eight o'clock, Lewis's shutters banged against the wall over my head and I jumped. I heard him come down the stairs and, whistling, light the burner under the coffeepot. His LSD seemed already to have disappeared, with sleep. I drew in a deep breath of fresh air and went into the kitchen. He looked surprised, and I contemplated him for a second, stupefied: so handsome, so young, so disordered, so gentle.

"I'm sorry about last night," he said quickly. "I'll never touch that foul stuff again."

"That's just it," I said in a dismal tone, and at last I sat down on a kitchen chair. The fact of having someone to talk to—even if it was he—strangely comforted me. He was watching the coffeepot, his manner extremely attentive, but just the same, there was something in my voice that made him turn his eyes toward me.

"What's going on?"

He seemed so innocent in his dressing gown, his eyebrows raised, that I began to have doubts. The fabric of coincidence, half-proofs, remarks that I had woven during the night was torn apart all at once.

"Lewis . . . it wasn't you who killed them, was it?"

"Who?"

The reply was, at best, discouraging. I did not dare look at him.

"All of them. Frank, Bolton, Lola."

"Yes."

I moaned and pushed back against the chair. He continued to speak in the same measured voice.

"But you mustn't worry about it. There's no trace. They won't bother us any longer."

He put a little more water in the coffeepot. I looked at him now, completely dumfounded.

"But really, Lewis . . . are you mad? You can't go around killing people, it just isn't done."

The phrase seemed weak to me, but I was so stunned that I couldn't find the right words. Besides, in tragic circumstances I can never manage to come out with anything but phrases from the convent and a polite education; I don't know why.

"If you only knew how many things 'aren't done,' yet people do them just the same . . . swindling others, bribing them, debasing them, abandoning them. . . ."

"But you mustn't kill them," I said firmly.

He shrugged his shoulders. I was expecting a tragic scene and this calm conversation disconcerted me. He turned to me.

"How did you know?"

"I thought about it. I thought about it all night long."

"You must be dead. Would you like some coffee?"

"No. 'Me,' I'm not dead," I said bitterly. "Lewis . . . what are you going to do?"

"Why, nothing. There was a suicide, a 'vile crime,' but without a clue, and a car accident. Everything's fine."

"And me?" I exploded, "and me? Am I going to live with a murderer? Am I going to let you kill people like that, at random, without doing anything about it?"

"At random? But, Dorothy, I only kill those who have hurt you or are hurting you. It isn't at random."

"What's wrong with you? Are you my bodyguard? Did I ask anything of you?"

He finally put down the coffeepot and calmly turned toward me.

"No," he said, "but I love you."

With that, my head began to turn, I slid from the chair, and with the aid of my insomnia, for the first time in my life I fainted.

I woke up on the sofa and saw Lewis; his expression, at last, was shocked. We looked at each other silently, then he handed me the bottle of scotch. Without turning my eyes from his, I took a swallow, then another. My heart began to beat normally again. And immediately rage overtook me.

"Ah, you love me? Really? That's why you killed poor Frank? and Lola? Why didn't you kill Paul while you were at it? After all, isn't he my lover?"

"Because he loves you. But if he tries to leave you, or harm you, I'll kill him, too."

"My God," I said, "you're crazy. Have you killed many before?"

"No, not before I knew you," he said. "Never. There was no reason. I didn't love anyone."

He jumped up, paced about the room, rubbing his chin. I had the impression that I was living in a nightmare.

"You see, until I was sixteen, I was more often beaten than anything else. They never gave me anything, never. And then, after I was sixteen, everyone wanted me, men, women—everyone, but on condition that, er . . . that . . ."

This prudish murderer exceeded all limits. I cut in.

"Yes, I see."

"Never anything, you understand. Never anything for nothing. Never anything free. Until you. I always thought, when I was in bed upstairs, that you would . . . well . . . some day . . ."

He blushed. I imagine I blushed, too. I was drifting between James M. Cain and Kathleen Norris. I was shattered.

"When I understood that it was out of kindness,

like that, I began to love you. That's that. I know you think I'm too young, that you prefer Paul Brett, and aren't interested in me, but I can still protect you. So that's that."

And that was that. As he said. That was that; that was that. I had put myself into a frightening nest of hornets. There was nothing I could do. I was lost. I had picked up on the road, from a ditch, a madman, a murderer, the victim of an obsession. Once again Paul had been right. Paul was always right.

"Do you hold that against me?" asked Lewis gently.

I did not even answer. Can one "hold something against" someone who has killed three people just to please one? The expression seemed a bit schoolboy-ish. I thought, or rather I pretended to think, for my head was completely empty.

"You know, Lewis, that it's my duty to turn you over to the police."

"If you wish," he said quietly.

"I should phone them immediately," I added in a weak voice.

He placed the telephone beside me and together we looked at it languidly, as though there were no cord attached to it.

"How did you do it?" I asked.

"For Frank, I made an appointment with him in your name at the motel, in a room reserved by telephone. I entered by the window. As for Bolton, I understood his case right away. I pretended to be willing. We immediately agreed to meet in a shady hotel. He was delighted. You can come and go as you like, with the key he gave me. No one saw me. For Lola, I spent the night unscrewing the bolts on the front wheels. That's all."

I could keep silent and throw Lewis out. But it would be like letting a lion loose in the streets. He would continue to follow me from afar and to kill, like a machine. I could demand that he leave the city, but he had signed a long contract and they would always find him, wherever he went. And I was not capable of turning him over to the police. I could never turn anyone over to the police. I was trapped.

"You know," said Lewis, "not one of them suffered. It was all very quick."

"Happily," I said bitterly. "You might easily have cut them up with a pocketknife."

"You know perfectly well that's not true," he said tenderly. He took my hand. Without thinking, I let him hold it for a moment. Then I remembered that the warm, thin hand that held mine had killed three people, and wondered why I was not more horrified. I firmly withdrew my hand from his.

"The boy yesterday, you wanted to kill him, too, didn't you?"

"Yes, but it would have been idiotic. I had stupidly taken a dose of LSD and I didn't know what I was doing."

"But without that . . . Lewis, do you realize what you've done?"

He looked at me. I scrutinized the green eyes, the perfect outline of his mouth, the black hair, the smooth skin; I looked for a sign of comprehension or a sign of sadism, and I found nothing. Nothing but a tenderness without limit for me. He looked at me as one looks at a child who has made a scene over nothing. I swear, there was indulgence in Lewis's eyes. That was the end: I began to cry. He took me in his arms, caressed my hair, and I did not stop him.

"Between the two of us," he murmured, "how we've cried since last night."

11

I had a liver attack, naturally. When the problem is serious, I always have a liver attack. This one lasted two days and had the advantage of giving me forty-eight hours during which I did not have to think. I came out of it dolefully and I determined to fix everything. That may seem very little, two days of nausea for three corpses, but only those who have never had a liver attack have a right to criticize me. When I got out of bed, my legs still weak, I could no longer face the idea of the slightest problem, that was all. In my mind, Lewis's murders were about equal in importance to my income tax return. What was more, the poor thing had spent two days at my bedside, equipped with compresses, basins, and camomile, obviously worried to death, and I could not bite the hand that fed me.

Nevertheless, I decided to put things straight with him, for once. As soon as I was able to swallow a steak and a strong whiskey, I called Lewis into the living room and made my ultimatum:

1) He would formally engage himself to kill absolutely no one without my permission. (Obviously, I would never give it, but I thought it clever to leave him some hope.)

2) He would stop taking his little sugar-lumps of LSD.

3) He would seriously try to find a place of his own to live.

On the third point, I felt less confident. Finally, however, he agreed to everything, his manner very serious. Then, not wanting to live with a sadist, I questioned him cunningly to see what effect the three crimes had had on him. He reassured me a little; not enormously, of course, but a little: they had had no effect at all. No sorrow, obviously, he said, because he had not known them; but no pleasure, either. It was that way each time. Otherwise he had no regrets, no nightmares; in short, he had no morals. I had begun to wonder, incidentally, what had become of mine.

Paul Brett had come by twice to see me during my illness, but I had refused to see him. One is never as nasty as during a liver attack. The idea of receiving my lover, with my yellow skin, dull hair, and puffed eyes, offended me. On the other hand, Lewis's presence did not bother me at all. Probably because there was nothing sensual between us. And then, he had told me he loved me, that famous morning, in such a way that I felt that I could be covered with impetigo and he would not care. As a woman, I was not sure if that was good or bad. That was what I tried to explain to Paul when he was slightly reproachful after my return to the office.

"You let Lewis care for you and you wouldn't even see me."

"I was hideous. If you had seen me you would never have looked at me again."

"It's funny, you know, it took me a long time to believe that there was nothing between you two, but now I'm sure. But, tell me, who does he sleep with?"

I had to admit that I had no idea. I had thought he had been in the arms of a starlet two or three nights, but it was just those nights that he was doing away with Bolton, or someone else. And yet Gloria Nash, the new star, the Number One now that poor Lola was dead, had noticed him and had even sent him an invitation to a party, to which she could not do otherwise than invite me, too. I asked Paul if he was going, and he said that he was.

"I'll come by for the two of you. I hope this little evening for three ends better than the other."

I sincerely hoped so, too.

"Just the same, I'm surprised such a simple fight made you so sick. Your liver attacks are well known in Hollywood, Dorothy. You had one when Frank left with Lola, one when Jerry threw you out after you had called him a dirty miser, and one when your poor, dear secretary fell out the window. But that was more serious, if I may say so."

"What do you expect, Paul? I'm getting old."

More serious . . . if he only knew. My God, if he only knew. I imagined his face for a second and began to laugh. I cried from laughter for five minutes at the mere idea. My nerves were certainly a bit frayed lately, too, and Paul became indulgent, patient, protective, American, virile, and even gave me his handkerchief to wipe away my runny mascara. At last I calmed down, muttered something stupid, and kissed him to keep him quiet. We were in my office. Candy had gone out, and he had become very tender. We agreed to return to his house, that very night, and I called Lewis to tell him to have dinner without me. (They were not shooting for a week.)

He was at the house, in very high spirits and amusing himself with the Rolls. I told him to be a good boy and laughter overtook me again. He promised not to budge until the next morning. With an impression of complete unreality, I went to have dinner at Chasen's with Paul, and must have met a hundred people, a hundred people who did not know. That stupefied me. It was only later, during the night, next to Paul, who slept with his head on my shoulder, as usual, and his right arm across my body, that I suddenly felt frighteningly alone and terrified. I had a secret, a mortal secret, and I had never had a personality for secrets. I remained awake like that until dawn, while five miles away, in his little bed, my sentimental murderer must have slept peacefully, dreaming of birds and flowers.

12

The evening of Gloria Nash's famous party, we were especially elegant. I put on a black beaded dress, bought in Paris at a crazy price, that showed my back to advantage—still one of my trump cards. Lewis in a dinner jacket, his black hair shining, was superb: he had the look of a young prince, with something of a faun. As for Paul, he represented the relaxed and elegant man of forty with his blond hair graying at the temples and his ironic eyes. I had resigned myself to crushing my beads between the two dinner jackets in the Jaguar when Lewis solemnly raised his hand.

"I have news for you, Dorothy."

I shuddered. But Paul began to laugh, like a conspirator.

"It's a real surprise, Dorothy. Let's follow him."

Lewis went to the garden, settled himself in the Rolls, and pushed on something or other. The Rolls made a soft, regular sound, backed up, and came to a stop in front of me. Lewis stepped out quickly, went around the car, and with a deep bow, opened the door. I was speechless.

"At least it managed to get this far," said Paul laughingly. "Don't be so surprised. Get in. Chauffeur, we're going to Miss Gloria Nash's, the star, Sunset Boulevard."

Lewis started off. Through the glass that separated us I saw in the rear-view mirror Lewis's look: enchanted, happy, childish, anxious for my pleasure. There were decidedly moments when life escaped me completely. In that gigantic cage, I found an old speaking-tube and I raised it to my mouth.

"Chauffeur, how is it that the Rolls is in running order?"

"I spent my week's vacation repairing it. For good."

I looked at Paul.

"He's been talking to me about it for three days," he said, smiling. "I believe he's twelve years old."

He in turn picked up the speaking-tube.

"Chauffeur, I recommend that you make an effort with the hostess tonight. Your indifference would be badly interpreted."

Lewis shrugged his shoulders, without answering. I desperately hoped everyone would be kind to me that evening, and that my criminal would not get any strange ideas. It had been trying during the last ten days; I had been constantly giving idyllic descriptions of people, sugar-coating all of my colleagues, all my friends, and presenting Hollywood, that infamous jungle, as a blooming paradise of young love. If a caustic remark about anyone slipped out, I immediately cited an imaginary service that individual had rendered to me three years before; in short, I would quickly become an idiot or go mad, if that had not already happened.

Gloria Nash was waiting for us at the door of her little thirty-two-room house. Everything was in order: spotlights in the garden, the swimming pool lit, giant barbecues and evening gowns. Gloria Nash is blond, pretty, and cultured. Unfortunately, she was born ten years (at least) after I was and she never stops reminding me of that fact in the most gracious way: sometimes by exclaiming, "But how do you manage, Dorothy, to have such a complexion? You must give me your secrets later"; sometimes by looking at me with an expression of wonder and stupefaction as though the fact that I could still stand alone at forty-five was prodigious. It was the second attitude that she chose that evening, and for an instant, under the look of amazement, I had the impression of being Tutankhamen disinterred, by chance, for the festivities. She immediately led me away to arrange my hair even though I had no need of it, but that was one of Hollywood's most boring and unchanging rituals— the women were expected to retire in compact little groups to comb their hair and powder their noses every ten minutes. The fact was that Gloria bubbled over with curiosity about Lewis, and asked me a thousand questions, which I evaded mechanically. She finally became annoyed, made several allusions which I ignored, and in despair, as we left her charming boudoir, decided to attack.

"You know, Dorothy, I have a deep affection for you. Yes, yes. Even when I was little, when I saw you in that film . . . er . . . anyway, someone has to warn you. There are queer stories going around about Lewis."

"What?"

My blood ran cold. I must have uttered a little cry in the guise of a question.

"How obstinate you are! . . . I must say he's madly seductive."

"There is nothing romantic between him and me," I said. "What sort of stories?"

"Well, they're saying . . . you know how people are here . . . they're saying that you and Paul and he . . ."

"What? Paul and him and me?"

"You're always between the two of them, so inevitably . . ."

All of a sudden I understood, and I began to breathe again.

"Oh, is that all?" I said gaily, as though it were only a childish joke (which was exactly the effect the thought of an orgy had on me, compared to the sinister truth). "Oh! Only that! That's not important."

And leaving Gloria perplexed, I went into the garden to see if Lewis, between two *petits fours*, had not found the time to stab someone who had not liked my beaded dress. No. He was calmly talking with one of the Hollywood gossip columnists. Relieved, I threw myself into the party, which was, incidentally, a great success. I met a number of my old suitors, all of whom tried to flatter me in their own way, complimenting me on my dress and my complexion until I began to think a good liver attack was the secret of rejuvenation. I should add that I've always remained on good terms with my former lovers, all of whom wear regretful expressions when they see me, murmur, "Ah! Dorothy, if only you had wanted . . . ," and allude discreetly to memories I do not always share with them, my memory fading, alas, with the passage of time. Paul kept watch on me from a distance, smiling to see me gamboling about like this, and once or twice I caught Lewis's eye—he seemed to be seriously besieged by Gloria. But I had decided not to worry about him. I wanted to enjoy myself. I had had enough emotions during the past few days. I wanted champagne, the fragrance of the California night, and the reassuring laughter of the good, brave, handsome Hollywood men who had never killed anyone, as far as I know, except in the movies.

I was happy as a lark, and slightly high, when Paul came to join me an hour later. Roy Dardrige, king of the Westerns, was plaintively explaining to me that I had ruined his life, four or five years before, and carried away by his emotions and an enormous quantity of martinis, he glared at Paul contemptuously, which left Paul completely indifferent. Paul took my arm and led me aside.

"Are you enjoying yourself?"

"Madly. And you?"

"Yes. To see you laughing, even from a distance."

The man was indisputably charming. I decided to marry him the very next day, since it meant so much to him. The only thing that stopped me from telling him so was my inflexible rule against voicing my ideas aloud at a party. Taking advantage of the shadow of a magnolia tree, I restricted myself to a tender kiss on the cheek.

"How's our little boy getting along?" I asked.

"Gloria looks at him the way a cocker spaniel looks

at a bone. She doesn't move an inch. His career seems to be assured."

That is, if he doesn't kill the butler, I thought quickly.

I decided to go and see what was happening—not in time: a scream came from the direction of the swimming pool, and I felt, for once, as happens in novels, my hair stand on end despite the lacquer that held it down.

"What is it?" I asked hoarsely. But Paul had already run toward the circle that was forming over there. I shut my eyes. When I opened them, Lewis was beside me, impassive.

"It's poor Rena Cooper. She's dead," he said calmly.

Rena Cooper was the columnist with whom he had been talking an hour earlier. I looked at him, horrified. True, Rena was not the symbol of human kindness, but in her detestable trade she was one of the best.

"You promised me," I said. "You promised."

"Promised what?" he asked, seemingly astonished.

"Promised not to kill anyone without asking my permission. You're a coward and your word means nothing. You're a born murderer; you can't be depended upon. I'm ashamed of you, Lewis. You fill me with horror."

"But . . . it's not me," he said.

"Tell that to someone else," I said bitterly, shaking

my head, "someone else. Who else would it be?"

Paul arrived, looking a bit sickened. He took me by the arm, asked why I was so pale. Lewis remained still, watching us, almost smiling; I could have slapped him.

"Poor Rena has had one heart attack too many," said Paul. "It's the tenth in a year. The doctor couldn't do a thing: she drank too much, and he'd warned her."

Lewis spread his hands wide and gave me the little mocking smile of someone unjustly accused. I began to breathe more easily. At the same time, I realized that for the rest of my life I could never read a death notice in the newspaper, or hear of anyone's dying, without suspecting him.

Naturally, the rest of the evening was a fiasco. Poor Rena was taken away in an ambulance and the rest of the guests left shortly afterward. I found myself at home, a little depressed, with Lewis. With a protective air, he gave me an Alka-Seltzer and suggested that I go to bed. I obeyed pitifully. It seems hard to believe, but I felt ashamed of myself. Morality is a strange thing; after too many fluctuations, I would never have the time to establish one before I too died —undoubtedly of a heart attack.

13

Then there was a marvelously calm period. Three long weeks passed without a hitch. Lewis worked, Paul and I, too, and we often dined together at the house in the evening. One sunny weekend we even went fifty miles down the coast to an isolated bungalow that a friend had lent Paul. It stood above the ocean, almost directly over the rocks, and we had to go down a little goat path in order to swim. The sea was rough that weekend, and Lewis and I, lazy, generally watched Paul swim alone. Like all well-preserved men of his age, he wanted to play the athlete, and it almost ended in catastrophe.

He was doing an elegant crawl, about thirty feet

from the shore, when he suddenly had a cramp. Lewis and I were in our bathrobes, eating toast on the terrace that overlooked the sea twenty-five feet below. I heard Paul call out feebly, saw him raise his hand, then an enormous wave passed over his head. I screamed and rushed down the little path. But Lewis had already taken off his robe and had dived, as simply as that, from twenty-five feet, risking to land on one of the rocks below. He reached Paul and returned in two minutes' time. When Paul had finished vomiting his salt water, and while I was stupidly tapping him on the back, I looked up and saw that Lewis was completely nude. God knows the number of nude men that I have seen in my life, but I felt myself blush. Our eyes met and Lewis jumped up and ran toward the house.

"My friend," said Paul a little later, once warmed up and livened by a grog, "my friend, you have courage. That dive . . . I think that without you, I wouldn't be here now."

Lewis groaned, embarrassed, naturally. I was amused to think that this boy passed his time saving and putting an end to human lives. His latest role pleased me more than the preceding one. Impulsively, I stood up and kissed him on the cheek. I might finally succeed in turning him into a good boy. It was a bit late, of course, if one thought of Frank, Lola, and so on, but there was still hope. I was less optimistic a little later when, taking advantage of Paul's absence, I congratulated him for what he had done.

"You know," he said coldly, "it makes no difference to me, personally, whether Paul lives or dies."

"Then why did you risk your life to save him?"

"Because you like him, and you would have suffered."

"If I understand you correctly, if Paul had not been my lover, you would have let him drown without lifting a finger."

"Exactly," he said.

I thought that I had never known so strange a conception of love. At any rate, his conception of love did not resemble any of the others I had inspired, where there was always a slight touch of possessiveness.

"But don't you have any . . . feeling, any affection for Paul, after three months?"

"You're the only one I love," he said in his serious way, "and no one else interests me."

"Exactly," I said. "Do you think that's healthy? Someone your age who . . . who attracts women should from time to time . . . I don't know . . . I . . ."

"Do you want me to fall into Gloria Nash's arms?"

"Hers or someone else's. Even from a simple health standpoint, I think it's better for a young man who . . . that . . ."

I stammered. What had come over me to start lecturing him like a doting mother? He looked at me sternly.

"I think people talk too much about that subject, Dorothy."

"Still, it's one of the most charming aspects of life," I protested feebly, reflecting all the while that I had devoted three quarters of my own time and thoughts to it.

"Not for me," said Lewis.

He had again, for an instant, that opaque look, that look of a wild, nearsighted animal that frightened me. I cut short the conversation. Outside of that, the long weekend had been very good for us. We were tanned, relaxed, and in very good spirits when we drove back to Los Angeles.

I was going to need it. Three days later they would be finishing Lewis's film, the famous Western, and Bill Macley, the director, invited a crowd to a cocktail party on the set to celebrate the end of the shooting. It took place in the fake village, all wood and flimsy store-fronts, where Lewis had dragged his feet all summer long. I got there about six o'clock, a little ahead of time, and found Bill in the fake saloon in the middle of the fake Main Street. I could see he was in a bad humor, worn out, and as rude as usual. His crew was preparing the next scene a bit farther down the street, and he was alone, sitting at a table, a mean look in his eyes. He had been drinking heavily lately, and they gave him only second-rate films now, which had made him more nervous than ever. He saw me and I was obliged to go up the two dusty steps that led to the saloon. He roared with laughter when he saw me.

"So, Dorothy? You've come to watch your gigolo work? It's his big scene today. Don't worry, he's a handsome little fellow; he won't cost you much for very long."

He was dead drunk, but I have very little patience, in spite of what one may think. I cordially called him a dirty bastard. He muttered that if I weren't a lady he would already have torn me apart, and I thanked him kindly to remember, even if it was a bit late, that I was just that.

"In any case, I'd like you to know that I'm engaged to Paul Brett," I added crisply.

"I know. Everyone says that the three of you do it together."

He burst into laughter and I was ready to throw something in his face—my handbag, for example— when I saw a form in the doorway. It was Lewis. I immediately regained my composure.

"Bill, honey, forgive me. You know I adore you, but my nerves are a bit worn."

Despite his condition, he was somewhat surprised, but he continued the conversation.

"It's your foreign blood; it goes a long way." He turned to Lewis. "You ought to know, shouldn't you?"

He punched Lewis on the shoulder and left. I laughed nervously.

"Good old Bill . . . he's not known for his finesse, but a heart of gold. . . ."

Lewis did not answer. He was unshaven, wearing a cowboy costume with a neckerchief knotted at his throat, and his thoughts seemed far away.

"At least," I added, "he's a good friend. What's the scene you're going to finish with today?"

"The murder," Lewis said tranquilly. "I kill the guy who raped my sister, the starlet. That took courage, I can assure you."

We went slowly toward the set where they were going to shoot the final scene. Lewis left me alone for ten minutes while he got himself ready. I watched. Even though the crew of technicians had arranged everything perfectly, Bill covered them with insults. It was evident that he had lost his self-control. Hollywood had destroyed him, too, at last. Hollywood and alcohol. The tables for the cocktail party had been placed outside and several thirsty people were already finishing their drinks. There must have been close to a hundred of us in the fake village, more or less grouped around the camera.

"Close-up of Miles," shouted Bill. "Where is he?"

Lewis walked calmly toward him, a Winchester in his hand, and he had the distant look that he always had when someone bored him.

Bill bent over, put his eye to the camera, and cursed loudly.

"It's lousy, all of it, lousy! Put the rifle to your shoulder, Lewis, shoulder, aim at me. . . . I want to see an expression of rage, do you understand, rage! . . . Don't look so idiotic, for God's sake: you're about to kill the bastard who raped your sister. . . . There, that's very good, that's it . . . very good . . . you pull the trigger . . . you . . ."

I did not see Lewis, he had his back turned to me. But he fired and Bill brought his two hands to his stomach, the blood spurted from between his fingers, and he fell. There was an instant when no one moved, then everyone rushed toward him. Lewis looked stupidly at the rifle. I turned and leaned against one of the false, musty-smelling walls and was sick to my stomach.

The police officer was very polite and very logical. It was evident that someone had replaced the blanks with real cartridges, it was evident that the person who had done it was among the thousand people who hated Bill Macley, it was also evident that it could not have been Lewis, who hardly knew him and seemed bright enough not to kill him in front of a hundred people. They were almost sorry for him, and attributed his silence, his grimness, to emotional shock: it is never funny to be the instrument of a crime. We left police headquarters about ten o'clock, with several other witnesses, and someone suggested that we have the drink that we had missed. I refused and Lewis followed me. We did not say a word until we had reached the house. I was completely exhausted, I was not even angry.

"I heard everything," Lewis said simply, at the bottom of the steps, and I did not answer. I shrugged my shoulders, took three sleeping pills, and went straight to bed.

14

The police officer was in the living room; he seemed
bothered. He was quite handsome, for that matter—
a little too thin, gray eyes, full lips.

"It's only a formality, you realize," he said, "but
you really know nothing more about the boy?"

"Nothing," I said.

"And he's lived with you for three months?"

"Oh, yes!" I replied, and with an apologetic shrug
added, "You must think that I lack curiosity."

He raised his black eyebrows and his face had the
same expression that I had often seen on Paul.

"That's the least I can say."

"You see," I said, "I feel that we know too much about the people we see often, and it's unpleasant. We know with whom they live, and how, with whom they sleep, what they like to think of themselves . . . I mean, too much. A bit of mystery is restful, isn't it? Don't you think so?"

Obviously he did not think it restful.

"It's one point of view," he said coldly. "A point of view that doesn't help my investigation. Of course I don't think he killed Macley deliberately. It even seems that he was the only one Macley treated decently. But he was the one who fired, just the same. When he comes before the judge, for the sake of his career, it would be better to paint as angelic a picture as possible."

"You should ask him," I said. "I know he was born in Vermont, and that's about all. Shall I awaken him or would you like another cup of coffee?"

It was the day after the murder. Lieutenant Pearson had gotten me out of bed at eight o'clock. Lewis was still asleep.

"I'd like another coffee," he said. "Mrs. Seymour, excuse me for putting the question so brutally: what is there between you and Lewis Miles?"

"Nothing," I said. "Nothing like what you might suppose. In my eyes, he's a child."

He looked at me and smiled suddenly.

"It's been a long time since I've wanted to believe a woman."

I laughed, flattered. In fact, I was horrified to let the poor man, representative of the law of my country, lose himself this way in this dreadful story. At the same time, I said to myself that if he had been pot-bellied, red-nosed, and brutal, my feeling of civic duty would not have been so strong. What was more, the effect of the sleeping pills had not completely worn off, and I was dead on my feet.

"The boy has a brilliant career before him," he said. "He's a remarkable actor."

I became rigid behind the pot of coffee.

"How do you know?"

"We had the rushes shown last night. You must admit that it helps, for a cop, to have a film of a murder—there's no need for a re-enactment."

He spoke to me through the kitchen door. I laughed foolishly and poured boiling water over my fingers.

"There was the close-up of Lewis's face: I must admit that it made me shiver," he continued.

"I think he'll be a great actor," I said. "Everyone says so."

With that, I grabbed the whiskey that was on the refrigerator and discreetly took a long drink, from the bottle. Tears came to my eyes, but my hands stopped trembling like two leaves in the wind. I returned to my living room and served the coffee properly.

"For your part, you see no obvious reason why young Miles should have wanted to kill Macley?"

"Not the least," I said firmly.

It was done; I was an accomplice. Not only in my eyes, but in the eyes of the law. The state prison was waiting for me. Well, so much the better: I would go to prison, I would find peace of mind. Suddenly I realized that if Lewis confessed, I would not only be an accomplice but, in the eyes of the public, the instigator of all the crimes, and I could end up in the gas chamber. I closed my eyes for an instant. Decidedly, fate was against me.

"Unfortunately, we don't see one either," said Pearson. "Excuse me, I meant to say unfortunately for us. Macley was a brute, it seems, and anyone could have entered where the properties are stored and changed the cartridges. There's not even a guard. It looks like it might be a long investigation. And I'm completely worn out these days."

He started to complain, but that did not surprise me. All the men I meet, whether they are cops, postmen, or writers, end up telling me their problems. It's a gift I have. Even my tax collector tells me about his conjugal mix-ups.

"What time is it?" someone asked sleepily, and Lewis, rubbing his eyes, appeared on the stairway. It was obvious that he had slept well and I was overcome with anger. He could kill people if he must, but at least he could welcome the police himself at dawn instead of purring on his pillow. I introduced him curtly. Lewis did not move a muscle. He shook hands with Pearson, asked me confusedly, with his crooked smile, if he might pour himself a cup of coffee, and I foresaw the moment when he would ask me sleepily if I were still angry with him because of the day before. That would have been the limit. I served him his coffee myself, he settled himself in front of Pearson, and the questioning began. That was how I learned that my gentle murderer came from a very good family, that he had had an excellent education, that all of his employers had been delighted with him, and that it was only his vagabond spirit, his need to wander, that had prevented him from having a brilliant career. I listened to it all, agape. The boy had been a perfect citizen, if I understood correctly, before he had fallen into the arms of Dorothy Seymour, *femme fatale* Number One, who had pushed him into committing four crimes. It was confusing—I, who had never killed a fly in my life without feeling guilty; I, to whom all the lost dogs, cats, and people rush. Lewis calmly explained that he had taken the Winchester from the cabinet where it was normally stored, and that he had not even thought of checking the rifle, having fired it in every direction during the eight weeks of shooting without a hitch.

"What did you think of Macley?" asked Pearson suddenly.

"A drunkard," said Lewis. "A poor drunkard."

"What effect did it have on you when he fell?"

"None," said Lewis coldly. "I was astonished."

"And now?"

"I still am."

"It didn't stop you from sleeping? The idea of having killed a man?"

Lewis raised his head and looked him straight in the eyes. I suddenly felt the perspiration on my forehead. He nibbled on one of his fingers, made an embarrassed gesture with his two hands.

"It didn't make any impression on me at all."

I knew that it was true, and to my stupefaction, I saw that it was what convinced Pearson of his innocence more than anything else. He stood up, sighed, and closed his note-pad.

"Everything you've told me has already been verified during the night, Mr. Miles, or almost everything. I'm sorry to have disturbed you, but it's regulations. Mrs. Seymour, thank you so much."

I accompanied him to the door. He muttered something about eventually having a drink together and I hurriedly accepted. I smiled sweetly at him as he drove off, a smile that made me feel as if I had fifty-two teeth. Trembling, I entered the house. Lewis was sipping his coffee, pleased with himself, and after the fright, I was overwhelmed by anger. I picked up a cushion and threw it in his face, and then a few other objects of little value that were scattered about my living room. I did it very quickly, without aiming much, and needless to say, a coffeecup broke against his forehead. He began to bleed profusely, and I broke into tears, once again. It was the second time in a month and in ten years.

I fell onto the sofa. I held Lewis's head in my hands. I felt the warm blood that dripped from my fingers, and I wondered why I had not had a presentiment, six months before, when I had held the same head in my hands, on a deserted road, in the light of the flames, and the same blood ran down my fingers. Still crying, I led him up to the bathroom, cleaned his cut with alcohol, and bandaged it. He said nothing; he seemed extremely downhearted.

"You were afraid," he said finally, incredulous. "You're not being reasonable."

"Not reasonable," I said harshly. "I have a man under my roof who has killed five persons. . . ."

"Four," he said modestly.

"Four . . . it's the same thing, and a police officer woke me up at eight o'clock in the morning . . . and you think it's unreasonable of me to be frightened. . . . That's the last straw."

"But there's no risk," he said gaily. "You saw for yourself."

"What's more," I added, "what's more . . . what about your model childhood? Good student, good employee, good everything. What do I look like? Mata Hari?"

He burst into laughter.

"I've told you, Dorothy. Before I knew you, I had

nothing, I was alone. Now that I have something of my own, I'm defending it, that's all."

"But you have nothing of your own," I said, exasperated. "I don't belong to you; I'm not your mistress, as far as I know. And you know very well that if we manage to escape the hangman, I intend to marry Paul Brett some day."

He stood up abruptly and turned his back to me.

"Do you think," he said, his voice distant, "that once you're married to Paul, I can no longer live with you?"

"Well, I don't think it figures among Paul's ideas. Of course, he likes you very much, but . . ."

I stopped suddenly. He had turned toward me and was staring at me with the same terrifying look that I now knew so well. The look of a blind man.

"No, Lewis, no!" I cried shrilly. "If you touch Paul, I'll never, never, see you again. Never again. I'll detest you, it will be the end, for you and me, the end."

The end of what? I wondered myself. He passed his hand across his forehead; he woke up.

"I won't touch Paul," he said, "but I want to be with you for the rest of my life."

He walked slowly up the stairs, like someone who has received a low blow, and I left the room. The sunshine gaily lit my poor garden, the Rolls, which had returned to its role as a statue, the hills in the distance, the entire little world that had been so peaceful and so bright. I shed a few more tears for my shattered life, and sniffing, returned to the house. I should get dressed. When I thought of it, Lieutenant Pearson was a very good-looking man, in spite of it all.

15

Two days later—two nightmarish days during which I spent most of my time crunching aspirins and even tried a tranquilizer, for the first time in my life, which incidentally put me in bad spirits and made me see suicide as a marvelous solution to my problems—two days later the storm and the flood arrived. I was awakened at dawn by the trembling of my bed, then the crashing of the water, and I felt a sort of bitter relief. The elements had entered the picture, Macbeth was not far away, the end was approaching. I went to the window; on the road, which had been transformed into a rushing river, I saw an empty car pass, followed by miscellaneous debris; then I made the rounds of the house and, from another window, I saw the Rolls caught in the torrent in the garden, like a fishing boat. The terrace was just above the water, about a foot. I congratulated myself, one more time, on not having cultivated my garden with loving care —there would have been nothing left of it.

I went downstairs. Lewis was at the window, enchanted. He hurried to offer me a cup of coffee with the imploring look he had worn since Bill Macley's murder, the eyes of a child who wants to be forgiven for a nasty joke. I immediately took a lofty attitude.

"Impossible to go to the studio today," he said gaily. "There's not a road open. And the telephone is cut off."

"Charming," I said.

"Luckily, yesterday at Tojy's I bought two steaks and some little cakes, those you like, made with candied fruit."

"Thank you," I said with dignity.

But I was very pleased. Not to work, to lounge about in a dressing gown and eat Tojy's delicious cakes . . . that was not so bad. Besides, I was in the middle of a fascinating book, full of forget-me-nots and daintiness, which was an agreeable change from murders and the reigning atmosphere.

"Paul must be furious," said Lewis. "He wanted to take you to Las Vegas this weekend."

"I'll ruin myself another day," I said. "Anyway, I

have my book to finish. And you, what are you going to do?"

"Make music," he said, "then I'll cook for you. Then we could play gin rummy, couldn't we?"

I could see that he was wildly happy. He had me at his mercy for the day; he had probably been rejoicing since early morning. I could not help but smile at him.

"Make a little music to start with while I read. I imagine the radio and television don't work either."

I have forgotten to point out that Lewis often played the guitar, slow and more or less melancholy music, quite strange, that he composed himself. I forgot because I know absolutely nothing about music. He picked up his guitar and began his chords. The storm raged outside, I drank my hot coffee in the company of my favorite murderer, I purred. Finally, to be happy so easily is terrible. Happiness is very binding; you can no more rid yourself of it than you can of a neurosis. You may be swamped by the worst troubles, you struggle, you defend yourself, you are obsessed by a single thought, and suddenly happiness hits you in the face, like a stone or a ray of sunshine, and you give in, all for the pleasure of being alive.

The day passed like that. Lewis won fifteen dollars from me playing gin, allowed me, thank God, to do the cooking, played the guitar, I read. I was not at all bored with him; he was light as a cat. While Paul, with his imposing physique, often tired me a little. I dared not imagine what it would have been like to spend the same day under the same conditions with Paul: he would have wanted to have the telephone repaired, start the Rolls, save the shutters, finish my screenplay with me, talk about people, make love, and heaven knows what all. . . . Action. Do something. But Lewis did not care. The house could leave its foundations, slip away like Noah's Ark, he languished there, happy with his guitar. Yes, when I think of it, it was a very gentle day in the middle of that raging storm.

When night fell, the elements redoubled their pranks. The shutters flew off in the wind, one after the other, like birds, with a lugubrious noise. Outside nothing could be seen. I could not recall having ever seen such a thing in the region. The Rolls banged against the wall, like a big dog at the door, furious at being left outside. I began to be frightened. I felt that God in his infinite bounty was being a bit harsh with his humble servant. Lewis, of course, was enchanted, overjoyed at the sight of my sheepish expression, and played the mock hero. Somewhat annoyed, I went to bed early, took what had become my habitual sleeping pills—after a lifetime of avoiding medicines—and tried to go to sleep. In vain. The wind was roaring now like a locomotive crammed with wolves, the house cracked from all sides, and about midnight, it cracked for good. Part of the roof literally flew off over my head and I was soaked by the water that poured in.

I screamed and by a stupid reflex buried my head under the dripping sheets, then rushed out of the bedroom into Lewis's arms. It was pitch dark. He pulled me toward him and, feeling our way, we entered his room, where the roof, miraculously, had withstood the elements. (Naturally it was my half of the house that had been decapitated and I who got the drenching.) Lewis had torn a cover from his bed and was rubbing me like an old horse, talking to me, as a matter of fact, in the same tone of voice that one uses with those quadrupeds when they are frightened, "There . . . there . . . it's nothing . . . it will pass. . . ." Afterward he went down to the kitchen by the light of his cigarette lighter to look for the bottle of scotch, and returned wet to the knees.

"The kitchen is full of water," he said briskly. "The sofa is floating in the living room along with the armchairs. I practically had to swim to catch this blasted bottle which happened to be floating, too. It's funny how happy-go-lucky objects seem when they change function. Even the refrigerator, so big and so clumsy, has taken itself for a cork."

I did not think it was so very funny, but I felt that he was doing what he could to entertain me. We were sitting on his bed, shivering and tangled in the covers, drinking from the bottle, in the dark.

"What are we going to do?" I asked.

"We're going to wait for daybreak," said Lewis calmly. "The walls are solid. All you have to do is lie down in my dry bed and sleep."

Sleep . . . the boy was mad. Nevertheless, fright and the alcohol had made my head spin and I lay down on the bed. He was sitting next to me; I distinguished his profile against the window and the wild clouds beyond. I began to think this night would never end, that I was going to die, and a sorrow, a childish terror, caught at my throat.

"Lewis," I begged, "I'm afraid. Lie down next to me."

He said nothing, but after a moment he walked around the bed and stretched out at my side. We were both lying on our backs and he smoked a cigarette, without speaking.

At that instant, the Rolls, pushed by a wave bigger than the others, crashed against our wall. The wall trembled with an atrocious noise and I threw myself into Lewis's arms. It was not a considered act, but I absolutely had to have a man take me in his arms and hold me tightly. Which is what Lewis did. But at the same time he brought his face toward mine and began to cover my forehead, my hair, my mouth with gentle kisses of an unbelievable tenderness. He murmured a sort of litany of love around my name, a litany that I did not understand very well, buried as I was in his hair and pressed against his body. "Dorothy, Dorothy, Dorothy . . ." His voice did not cover the noise of the storm. I did not move, I was warm against his warm body, I thought of nothing else, unless, confusedly, that it was bound to have finished like that, and that it was of no great importance.

Only it could not finish like that and I suddenly realized it. And at the same time I understood Lewis and the reason for his acts. And the murders and his mad, platonic love for me. I sat up quickly, too quickly, and he immediately let go of me. We did not move for an instant, both of us petrified, as though a serpent had unexpectedly slid in between us, and I no longer heard the wind, only the deafening beat of my heart.

"So you know," said Lewis slowly. . . .

And he lit his cigarette lighter. I saw him in the light of the flame, perfectly handsome, so alone, more alone than ever. . . . I held out my hand to him, overcome by a dreadful pity. But he already had his blind look, and he no longer saw me, he dropped the lighter, and his two hands were at my throat.

I am absolutely not suicidal, but for an instant I had the desire to let him continue, I don't know why. The pity, the tenderness that I felt propelled me toward death as though toward a refuge. That was probably what saved me: I did not fight back for a second. The pressure of Lewis's fingers reminded me that life was the most precious thing that I owned. I calmly began to talk to him, with what threatened to be my last breath.

"If you wish, Lewis . . . but it hurts me. I've always loved life, you know, and I love the sunshine and my friends and you, Lewis. . . ."

The pressure of his hands continued. I began to suffocate.

"What are you going to do without me, Lewis? You're going to be bored. . . . Lewis, my darling, be nice, let me go."

And, abruptly, his hands left my throat and, sobbing, he threw himself against me. I placed his head comfortably on my shoulder and for a long moment caressed his hair without saying a word. Several men have collapsed on my shoulder in my life, and nothing moves me or inspires more respect in me than those sudden and savage masculine sorrows, but none of them had inspired such tenderness in me as the sadness of this boy who had almost killed me. I had renounced all logic, thank heaven, a long time ago.

Lewis went to sleep quickly, exhausted at the same time as the storm, and I kept him all night long on my shoulder, watching the sky become pale, the clouds disappear, and finally an insolent sun rise over a ravished land. It was one of the most beautiful nights of love I had known in my life.

16

The next day, just the same, I had several blue marks on my neck and they made a most horrid impression. I mused a long time before the mirror, for once, then reached for the telephone.

I told Paul that I accepted his offer of marriage and he seemed overjoyed. Then I announced my decision to Lewis, told him that I would probably go to Europe on my honeymoon, and that he could take care of the house during my absence.

The marriage ceremony lasted ten minutes, with Candy and Lewis as witnesses. After which I closed my luggage, took Lewis in my arms and held him there, promising him that I would return soon. He promised me to be good, to work hard, and to weed around the Rolls every Sunday. Several hours later, I was flying to Paris, and as I watched through the window the silvery wings cutting through the banks of blue-gray clouds, it seemed to me that I was coming out of a nightmare. Paul's hard, warm hand was holding mine.

We had planned to stay only one month in Paris. But Jay sent me a telegram asking me to go to Italy to help another poor slave like myself who was having trouble with a script. Paul had people to see in London, where RKB was setting up another production company. For six months we shuttled continually between Paris, London, Rome. I was delighted: I met a lot of people, saw my daughter often, I swam in Italy, celebrated in Paris, in London, I renewed my wardrobe from head to foot, Paul was excellent company, and I loved Europe as much as ever. From time to time I received a letter from Lewis in which he spoke childishly of the garden, the house, the Rolls, and complained timidly of our absence. The publicity caused by the death of Macley had revived interest in his first film. Charles Vaught, a very good director, had been hired to reshoot the film, in which certain scenes seemed to have been completely botched, so Lewis had returned to his cowboy suit. His role appeared to have been built up a little. But he wrote of that in an almost plaintive way, and I was taken aback when, three weeks before our return, I heard that the film was marvelous and the young leading man, Lewis Miles, had a good chance to be awarded an Oscar for his remarkable interpretation.

That was not the last surprise I was to get. When we landed at Los Angeles, I found Lewis at the airport. He threw his arms around my neck, then around Paul's, like a child, and began to complain bitterly. "They" never stopped pestering him, "they" offered him contracts about which he understood nothing, "they" called night and day on the telephone, "they" had even rented an enormous house with a swimming pool for him. He seemed distraught and furious. If I had not arrived that very day, he would have fled. Paul roared with laughter, but I thought Lewis did not look well and that he had lost weight.

The big evening, the presentation of the Oscars, was the next day. All Hollywood was there, dressed to the teeth, made-up, glittering, and Lewis had his Oscar. He walked casually onto the stage, and in a philosophical mood I saw three thousand people enthusiastically applaud a murderer. One becomes accustomed to everything. After the Oscars had been awarded, there was a big party, organized by Jay Grant, at Lewis's new house. Jay, manifestly proud of himself, showed me around: the closets crammed with new suits for Lewis; the garages where the new cars, more or less offered free to Lewis, slept, the apartments where Lewis would sleep, where Lewis would receive. He followed us, mumbling.

"Have you brought over your old blue jeans yet?" I asked, turning toward him.

He shook his head, horrified. For the hero of the evening, he seemed singularly unconcerned. He confined himself to following me step by step, refusing, despite my admonitions, to take care of his guests, and I began to notice certain glances, hear certain remarks that pressed me to accelerate our departure. I took Paul by the arm, taking advantage of a moment when someone else was monopolizing Lewis, and whispered to him that I was tired.

We had decided to live at my house, at least temporarily, because Paul's apartment was in the center of the city and I preferred the country. It was almost three in the morning when we discreetly left for the car. I looked at the enormous house, all lit up, the shimmering water in the swimming pool, the guests' silhouettes in the windows, and I said to myself that a year before, barely a year, we had been returning home on this same road when a young man jumped in front of the car. What a year! . . . Anyway, it had all ended well—except, of course, for Frank, Lola, Bolton, and Macley.

Paul backed out expertly between two Rolls—new ones—and slowly drove off. And exactly as a year before, a young man, his arms widespread, flung himself against the car, in the glare of the headlights. I gave a stupefied cry and Lewis came running to my side of the car, opened the door, and took hold of my hands. He was shaking like a leaf.

"Take me home," he said in a broken voice. "Take me with you, Dorothy, I don't want to stay here."

He pressed his head against my shoulder, then raised it again, breathing deeply like someone who has received a blow.

"But look, Lewis," I stammered, "your home, it's here now. And all those people waiting for you . . ."

"I want to go back home," he said.

I cast an amazed glance at Paul. He laughed quietly. I made a last try.

"Think of poor Jay, who has gone to so much trouble. He'll be furious if you leave like that."

"I'll kill that one," said Lewis, and I flinched.

I immediately moved over and Lewis fell onto the seat beside me. Paul started off and we were once again, we three, on the road, and I was completely dazed. Just the same, I gave a little moral lecture to Lewis, explaining that it was all right for tonight because he was nervous, and with reason, but that he had to return to his house in two, or perhaps three days, that people would not understand why he was not living in that marvelous house, and so on.

"I could live at your house and we could all go over there to swim," he said reasonably.

With that he fell asleep on my shoulder. We almost had to carry him out of the car when we arrived; we took him up to his little bedroom and put him to bed. He opened his eyes slightly, looked at me, smiled, and went back to sleep, a blissful expression on his face.

We entered our bedroom, Paul and I, and I began to undress. Then I turned to Paul.

"Do you think we'll have him for a long time?"

"For a lifetime," said Paul casually. "You know very well."

He smiled. I protested feebly but he cut me short.

"Aren't you happy that way?"

"Yes," I said, "very."

And it was true. Obviously I would have trouble stopping Lewis from killing people, from time to time, but with a little supervision and luck . . . well, "we would see." This diabolical formula soothed me, as always, and humming to myself, I headed for the bathroom.